M.A. MOLLENKOPF

The Mindjack Murders

Detective Jack Stewart Investigates

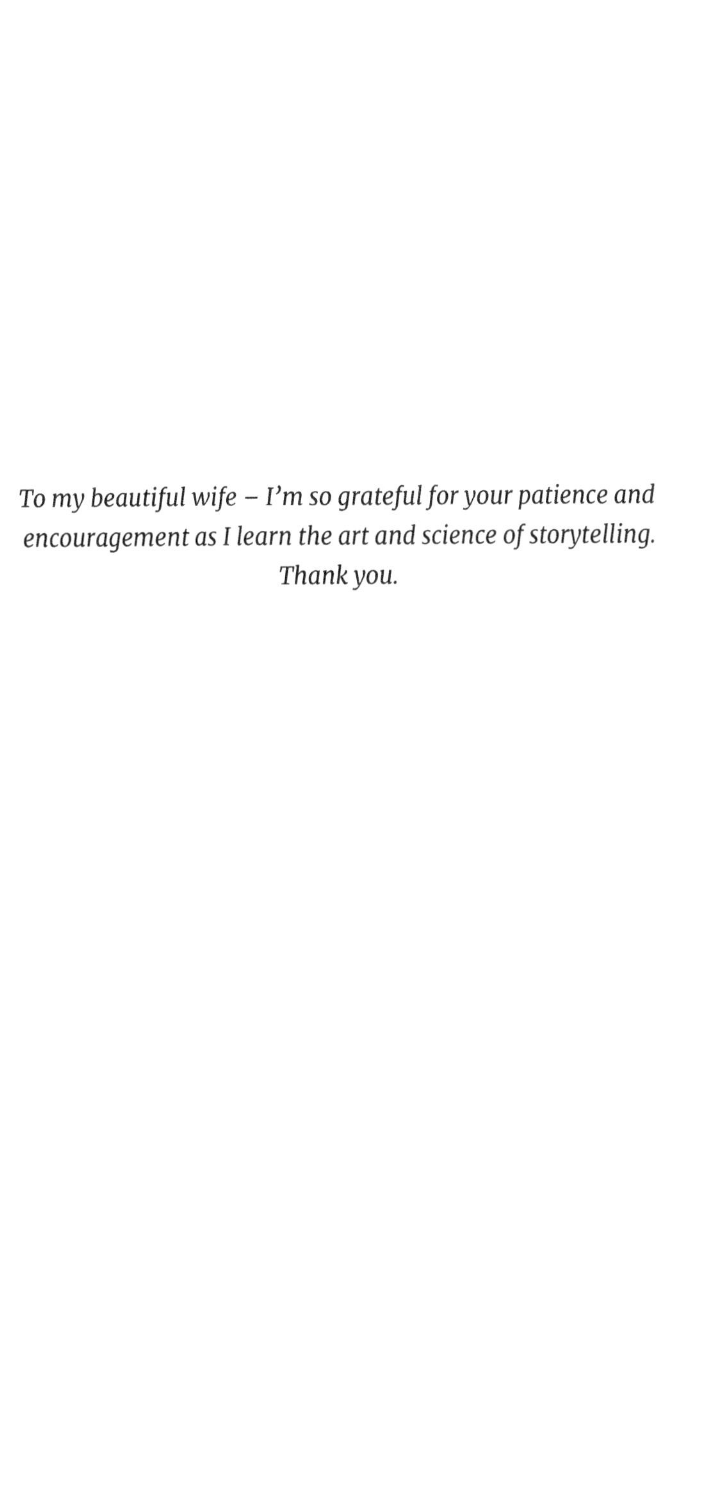

To my beautiful wife – I'm so grateful for your patience and encouragement as I learn the art and science of storytelling. Thank you.

Contents

Chapter 1

He looked normal enough. Well, except for those eyes.

"So you're...how old?" I asked again politely as my temper started to brew.

"Does it matter how old I am? Your boss called me an alien. I'm not an alien," he replied in a low, deadpan voice.

"I need a number. As you can see, I'm filling out a report and would appreciate your help," I said with growing irritation in my voice.

"Okay, I'm fifty."

Egad, I hate these spurious interrogation tasks. I was ten minutes from going home, I thought. "I'm going to need a few more details. As we seem to have gotten off on the wrong foot, maybe it's best if we start over. What is your name?" I said, smiling.

"My name is Jacobs. Q. Jacobs."

"Great, Mr. Jacobs. See, that was easy. Let me write that down here. What does the Q stand for?"

"Quartz."

"Quartz? Okay, that's unusual. May I address you as Quartz?"

"Sure, that's fine."

"Okay, Quartz. I'm going to need an address. Where do you live? Where are you from?"

"I was born in Cortropolis."

"Cortropolis? Where is that? Is it in the States? Europe?"

"I don't remember exactly. I haven't been there since I was a child. It's down near South America, Argentina, I think. I presently reside at 1010 North State Street, downtown."

"Okay, you live at the plaza and are from South America, good enough. Where do you work?"

"I work at Storm and Shield Holdings."

Grrr. Is this guy going to make me probe for every damned detail? I thought. "Please feel free to provide any additional details as we go. What do you do at Storm and Shield Holdings?"

"I'm a consultant."

Oh for... "Really? No shit. Come on, Quartz, give me something to work with, or my boss is going to keep us here all night. Is that what you want?"

"No, I'm ready to go. I'm not an alien."

Well, shit, I thought. *Going to be a long night.* There was a knock at the door. "Come in," I said.

"Chief Borland wants to see you, Detective."

"Great." I half smiled as I rose from my chair. I headed toward the door. "Excuse me for a moment, Quartz," I said. "Please don't go anywhere."

"Funny. I'm still cuffed to this chair, ya know."

I glanced back at Quartz with a slight frown. "Like I said, stick around."

***

"Chief, you wanted to see me? I haven't gotten very far with the suspect you asked me to interview. I don't think he's an alien though. He's got a driver's license, Social Security number, and such."

"Come in, Jack. Shut the door and take a seat."

"Yes, sir," I said as I entered the room and noticed the chief pacing about his tiny office. When the chief paced, it usually meant that he was in deep thought.

The chief stopped pacing and then turned to look at me as he spoke in his low, gravelly voice.

"What I'm about to say, Jack, is off the record."

Whoa, I thought. I tried carefully, glancing around the room to see if there were any active cameras or recording devices. I decided not to look too hard, as he seemed dead serious.

"Yes, sir. Off the record."

"He's a suspect in the Jessica Frontage case. For clarification, I never suspected he was an illegal alien."

"What are you saying?"

"I meant *alien*, as in not from Earth. I know it sounds crazy, but hear me out. Storm and Shield Holdings is a really old company with ties everywhere, and I mean *everywhere*. Several employees have unusually long backgrounds. One of them is over one hundred and twenty years old and doesn't look a day over forty. And there's these devices." The chief opened a shoebox containing a few apparently heavy items. The box's structure shifted around as its contents rolled from corner to corner.

I gave the chief a puzzled look. "Okay, Chief, I'll do a deep dive of Storm and Shield. What's got you rattled, boss? That suspect? What are you thinking?"

"I can't pin it down yet, but be careful, Jack. I know how this sounds. Their eyes don't look normal, and they all have four fingers on each hand. There's something consistently different about them. No trace of family, no parents. It's all too strange." The chief resumed pacing about the office.

I've never seen the chief so agitated before, I thought.

"I'm placing you on a special assignment. Do not... "

The chief paused as he apparently decided to rephrase his statement.

"Please don't tell anyone about this. If anything happens to me, I want you to report your findings discreetly to this woman. She's in charge of a special team that investigates these sorts of things. They are onto something big, but they won't share any details with us."

The chief stepped toward me, and I took the business card and the shoebox from him and glanced at the name on the card.

Amanda Seward

Officer In Charge

Special Action Group

"That box contains evidence that I think will prove they're aliens. *Actual freakin' aliens, Jack.* I want you to take that box and do some research on the ball-looking thing in particular. Don't use our lab. I want you to use the bureau's lab downtown."

I opened the box and looked inside. "Got it, sir. Weird. It looks like an orb from a science fiction movie...thing. It's very heavy," I said as I lifted the orb and then let it fall with a light *thunk* back into the box.

"Yes, it's very strange. It'd be best if you didn't mess with it here. It's easily turned on, and it gets warm and blindingly bright immediately. I don't want us to accidentally blow the place up."

Noted, I thought sarcastically as I nodded at the chief and put the lid back onto the shoe box, firmly attaching it into place.

The chief stopped pacing and acted as though he'd had an epiphany. "I have to go and run down a lead. Contact me immediately if you find anything. I think time is precious in this investigation. The murder suspect you are interviewing, well, he's one of those super-old employees of Storm and Shield Holdings. His prints were found at the murder scene and on the property in that box. A couple of months ago, I saw him get hit by a car with my own eyes. Not a glancing blow but a direct collision while he was crossing the street. *POW!* I saw the whole accident, so I pulled over and phoned emergency services. I stayed there until the EMTs took over. He was stable, so the EMTs took him to Southern General."

The chief stopped then pivoted toward his desk to grab his car keys and continued, "I was curious, so the next day I went to check on him at the hospital. Son of a bitch was never admitted, never checked in." He rubbed his temples in frustration and then continued, "The next day, I camped out in front of Storm and Shield, and sure as I'm telling you this story, he showed up for work promptly at 7:00 AM. Not a scratch. That got me looking at him and a couple of the other employees there. I pulled what I could find on their backgrounds and realized the company is really old. Lots of employees but no information about them. No social media, wedding announcements, none of the normal stuff. Sorry, I really need to run. Be careful, Jack. I should be back tomorrow so we can sync."

And just like that, the chief opened his office door and walked out. I looked at the door swung wide open. I exhaled deeply as I looked down at the shoebox and pondered my next steps. *Murder and aliens. Sheeez. Coffee. I definitely need coffee.* I figured I'd grab a cup before I headed back to this Quartz guy.

With shoebox in hand, I went to find a cup of Joe.

Chapter 2

I clumsily opened the interrogation room where Quartz was sitting. Clumsily because I had a cup of black coffee in each hand and a shoebox under my arm.

"Quartz, do you like black coffee?"

"I do. I also like drinking it *at home*," he replied tersely.

I set his cup down on the table, spilling a little and in the process dropping the shoebox on the floor.

Something in the shoebox made a loud, high-pitched whining sound, as if an expensive tuning fork had struck something really hard.

A deputy poked his head into the room and looked around quizzically. "Detective, is everything all right in here?"

"Yes, we're fine. I dropped a box is all. Do me a solid and set this on my desk. The office cleaners were in there a few minutes ago, or I'd have done it myself."

The deputy peered back at me. He looked over at Quartz and then said, "Well, I'm not your box delivery bitch, but happy to help, Detective."

I looked back at the deputy with a furrowed brow of curiosity. I didn't quite know what to make of that "box bitch" comment, so I shifted to a default smile and said thank you as I handed him the box.

The door closed, and I turned to face Quartz.

Whoa! He has a much different look on his face now, I thought.

He appeared stiff and immobilized with those deep-set green eyes wide open. The comfortable, irritated "Hey, I'm an innocent man" smirk was gone. I couldn't pin it down yet, but I'd say it was a look of concern or even fright.

"Sorry about that, Quartz," I said. "I'm all thumbs without regular coffee ingestion."

Quartz's eyes were locked onto my eyes like two lasers. He was definitely parsing through some decision tree in that brain of his.

I moved slowly to sit back down at the table. He scooted backward an inch as I took my seat across the table from him. "Hey, Quartz. Relax," I said as I looked across the table at him. He finally relaxed a bit and shifted in his seat after nearly a minute of being frozen, staring at me.

Quartz looked down at the table. "Detective, I took the liberty of filling out your report."

I looked down at the report and turned it so I could read it. "Hmm. Okay, this looks pretty good, Quartz. Thank you. I'm curious though. What's got you spooked?"

Quartz kept his eyes locked onto mine and spoke flatly. "It's late. I need to go, unless you are charging me with a crime."

I stared directly at Quartz for a few seconds, realizing he must have recognized that tuning fork sound that rang out when I dropped the shoebox. *Shit, I wonder where Chief got those items,* I thought.

Quartz must have concluded his thought process, as his posture relaxed a degree in his chair. His face shifted into a friendlier half smile. "It's always good to have friends in the community, Detective, friends who can help when others aren't being…quite so helpful."

I considered his words carefully. I knew what he really meant, but to avoid revealing that I understood, I decided to play dumb. "Okay, Quartz, so if I can get you out of here, we can be friends? I'll take that. And I do appreciate you filling out the report for me. Indeed, a timesaver." I smiled gently as I removed the handcuff keys from my pants pocket, stood, and stepped over to Quartz's chair. I unlocked the cuffs, and he immediately stood up, rubbing his wrist a little. *Wow, he's tall,* I thought as I took a step back and smiled.

"Have a good evening, Quartz," I said, stuffing the keys back into my pocket before checking my cellphone for messages.

Quartz stepped around the other side of the desk and went toward the door, pausing at it. "Good evening, Detective."

Quartz wasted no time leaving.

Deputy Schultz popped back into the interrogation room with the shoebox under his arm. "Well, did it work, Detective? Did he recognize the sound?"

"Yes," I responded quietly as I thought through the next steps. "It certainly did." I stepped toward Schultz and said, "Thank you, Shultzy, appreciate your help. You are the man. Hey, what was all that 'box bitch' wording?"

Schultz smiled broadly as he handed the box back to me. "You're welcome, Detective. Making it look legit, sir. You know, adding realism. Unfortunately, I need to run. I have an errand or two to handle. See you tomorrow."

"Right. Thanks. I'm not far behind you." I collected my things from the office and headed to my car. A thousand thoughts flew through my mind as I tried to pull together what could be going on here. I checked my phone one more time. No messages from Chief Borland. *That stinks. Maybe I need a little sleep.*

I got into my car and drove home, thinking the whole way about the chief, the Special Action Group, the shoebox items, and of course Storm and Shield Holdings.

I rolled into my driveway, disarmed my alarm system, and opened my garage door with the remote. *Did I leave the garage light on? I never do that!* I parked the car, pulled my Glock out of its holster, and quietly exited the vehicle. I crept into my house, very tired but ready for action.

At low volume emanating from the living room was the play-by-play announcer for the Cincinnati Reds providing game updates over my trusty AM radio. I remembered the Reds had played the Chicago Cubs earlier and was hoping to catch the rebroadcast.

The kitchen looked undisturbed as I crept through it, heading toward the living room where, as it came into view, I noted unusual lights glowing softly.

"You need a better security system, Jack. And what's with the AM radio? Who uses them anymore?"

"Damn it, Chief, you have to be careful, you know, breaking into other police officer's houses. Especially well-armed police officers. *Like me*," I relaxed and looked around the immediate area, scanning for anomalies.

"I'm heading to Storm and Shield first thing tomorrow. I want you to back me up. But don't go in with me. I want you to overwatch from the street."

"Chief, first, it's already tomorrow. Second, I'd like to get some sleep. Are you sure we need to act so fast? I need some time to sort out what's happening here."

The chief got up out of my recliner and strode over to me. He rested his right hand on my left shoulder.

"Maybe, Jack. Maybe we do have time, but I'm still going in

the morning. If you could show up around 8:30, it would be good. By the way, there's a cheeseburger in the microwave with your name on it. You're welcome. Sounds like the Reds won tonight. Good game, Reynolds nearly pitched a no-hitter."

I smiled. "Chief, you taught us not to eat junk food like that, especially this late at night. And please don't spoil the game, my morning festivities revolve around coffee and baseball stats."

He smiled and walked over to the front door. "Sometimes a cheeseburger can be therapeutic. Oh, I also left you two reports from Amanda Seward. That's the gal over at the—"

"The Special Action Group. Yeah, I'm tracking who she is and what they are. Well, sort of."

"Good," the chief said as he smiled broadly and maneuvered out the front door. "Have a good night."

"Nite, Chief."

I walked over and locked the front door, watching out my front window as the chief walked down the sidewalk to his car, which was parked down the street.

Curious, I headed over to the microwave, opened it up, and grabbed the bag. I peeked into the bag, and my nose thought, *Whoa, I'm not that hungry.* I chucked the bag into the trash.

I put a cup of water into the microwave and punched up a couple of minutes. As the microwave heated my tea water, I skimmed the reports. *Wow, this sort of thing is new for us here in Wellspoint*, I thought.

The first report described a set of dead bodies that were found about twelve weeks prior in a car submerged in Wellspoint Lake. There was no indication that the car was struck or pushed off the road, no guardrail damage, skid marks on the pavement, or anything similar. The bodies weren't mutilated or disfigured, but they did have suspicious marks and wounds around the skull region, and all had severely bloodshot eyes from numerous burst vessels. The second report described how a homeless man was attacked, taken hostage by a policeman, and claimed to have some procedure done on his brain and performed by aliens, *of course.* It struck me as odd that the description of the policeman resembled Chief Borland a little, including the W-shaped birthmark on his right hand.

Shit, please tell me this is not connected to Storm and Shield, I thought.

I downed a half cup of green tea as I read the reports and decided it was time to get some sleep.

I dropped onto the bed and crashed hard. *Tomorrow will be a good day*, I thought.

Chapter 3

I woke up with a sore throat. *Must have snored last night.* I glanced at the ceiling and noted the current time being projected by my bedside clock, 6:07 AM.

Whoa. Gotta move, I thought. I jumped into the shower and started getting cleaned up, thinking hard about the condition of the dead bodies as described in the report. I wanted to show up in time to get ahead of the chief going into the Storm and Shield facility so I could get an understanding of what was going on.

I poured coffee from the pot and gave it a deep sniff. *Yep, it smells wonderful. Man, I love coffee.*

Keys in hand, I grabbed the reports off the counter and stuck them in my leather satchel.

Thirty minutes later, around 7:20 AM, I parked across the street from the Storm and Shield front door and then backed down the street about fifty meters to avoid being in the direct line of sight of anyone entering or exiting through the front door.

As I sat in my car, a few pedestrians passed by. About fifteen minutes later, a car pulled up to the Storm and Shield front door. One adult male exited the building and stepped into the car. He was dressed conservatively in business attire. He had a briefcase, and I took a few photos with my phone.

I made a few notes about the vehicle, including the license plate number. *Probably an Uber or similar transportation service,* I thought.

Nothing else really happened until my brain said, *It's 0830 AM. Where's the chief?*

Growing restless, I swallowed the last of my coffee, placed the cup back in the holder, and skimmed through the baseball stats on my tablet computer. Chief was right; Cincinnati played well yesterday. *About time.*

I was about to start my car and drive away when my peripheral vision caught motion near the front door. Turning my head to look toward the door, I could see that both doors had flown open. I was in time to see a male exit through the door on the left of the opening. Once he hit pavement, he turned left and started running up the street in the opposite direction from where I was parked.

What the hell... Is that the chief? It was.

Two burly males pursued the chief out the front door and down the street.

I opened my car door, stepped out, slammed the door shut, and sprinted across the street to the front door of Storm and Shield. I stopped at the open double doors, peered inside, and unholstered my pistol. I thought about pursuing the chief, but now may be the best chance to check out Storm and Shield without a warrant. "Police! I'm coming in. I say again, this is the police. I'm coming in."

I stepped carefully through the wide-open double doorway, glancing around and down the green-tiled staircase to a rather wide white-tiled hallway beneath it that appeared to have several rooms connected to it. I didn't see anyone.

I walked carefully down the stairs, watching for movement

in the main hallway below. When I reached the bottom of the stairs, I looked across the cavernous hallway and noticed a red-tiled, short staircase that connected to another set of double doors.

The doors were open, and I could faintly see several huge pieces of equipment with blinking lights on them in the dimly lit room. *Looks like a lab of some kind.*

"Stop! You, get out of here!"

A very tall male who looked a lot like Quartz ran down the white-tiled hallway toward me.

I lowered my pistol and raised my left hand above my head, palm open. "I'm Detective Stewart, a police officer. I'm investigating some unusual activity in the area," I said.

The tall male walked right up to me, clearly unafraid. *Whoa, he is tall, like Quartz. I'm guessing 6' 8".*

"Officer, I'm going to have to ask you to get the hell out of my building unless you have a search warrant or are willing to shoot me."

He had deep-set, large green eyes like Quartz and a very intimidating physique, also like Quartz. I noted two people ascending the red-tiled staircase out of the dimly lit room. We both glanced at them and back at each other. They closed the double doors behind them, walked up the red-tiled staircase, then walked down the hallway, stopping next to the gentlemen who resembled Quartz as if they wanted to discuss something with him.

I took a few steps to the rear, keeping my eyes locked on the big man, and said, "Okay, it seems like everything here is under control." I carefully started stepping back up the stairs. I stepped sideways so I could keep my eyes on the people below while periodically glancing up the stairs toward the wide-open, double-doored exit. Footsteps echoed in the distance. Suddenly, the two males who chased after the chief entered through the doorway above me and looked surprised to see me sidling up the green stairs toward them. One of them pulled a pistol from a jacket holster.

"Gentlemen, this is Detective Stewart. He's leaving," said the tall man who resembled Quartz.

I glanced back up the stairs to my left. *Yep, those qualify as henchmen. Armed henchmen,* I thought. I kept sidestepping up the stairs as one of the two men walked calmly down the stairs on the other side of the center-positioned handrail. He walked right by and continued over to the group.

"Detective, my name is Flint. I'm the business manager here at Storm and Shield. I'm not sure what you are investigating, but if you need to discuss any ongoing investigations you believe involve Storm and Shield, simply phone and ask for me by name. No need to come all this way for nothing."

I glanced up at the man standing in the doorway between me and the street. He had a pistol in his right hand, and I was getting concerned about departing without a firefight. *Great, and me with no place to get cover*, I thought. I decided to keep moving. Glancing back down at Flint, I replied, "Flint, sorry to have disturbed you today. I'll be on my way." I took several more side steps up the stairs and finally reached the top. I stood in the exit entryway next to the rather large man standing there.

Damn, he was big.

Flint said, "Charlie, come on down and let Detective Stewart move along."

Charlie looked down at me as if sizing me up. He turned and started down the stairs. Once down the stairs, he kept walking along the massive hallway, past Flint, obviously headed for a destination deeper within the building.

"Detective, we *are* looking for a piece of equipment that was stolen from our lab. A sphere-shaped device. It is very heavy, shiny, and extraordinarily valuable. If you see it, can you please let me know?"

I looked down the stairwell at Flint and the two men standing next to him. Flint looked seriously pissed off.

"Okay, Flint, I'll look around for a device that matches that description, not much to go on though," I said.

Flint replied matter-of-factly, "Okay, for example, if it strikes something hard, the device emits a high-pitched whine, like a tuning fork. It's quite delicate, so I'd recommend being very careful with it. It holds a great deal of energy. It is, you understand, an important piece of Storm and Shield property."

I thought about the small device sitting in a cardboard box in my car and wondered if the device was "missing" because Chief Borland took it, or maybe someone working with him had removed it from the offices of Storm and Shield.

Without saying another word, I holstered my pistol, turned, and walked briskly back toward my car.

I got into my police car and drove off, not sure where I was headed. I phoned the chief. No answer. I contacted the police dispatcher and asked for a patch through to Chief Borland via police radio and was told that the chief had taken today off and would return tomorrow.

Well, damn.

I looked down at the shoebox on the passenger side's floor and considered how I could get across town to retrieve the items examined by the bureau's lab personnel and then return to the station to perform some badly needed research on Storm and Shield. I have a connection at the lab, and I was pretty certain she'd help me without asking a bunch of questions.

I needed to know what was going on there, and I surmised that understanding that might be key to help resolve some of my questions.

The chief is certainly onto something here. These guys are definitely strange. Their physiques are different. They are all at least 6' 6". They all have four-fingered hands, and all their eyes are huge and so deeply inset in the sockets. Weird.

Along the way to the station, I stopped to collect my thoughts. I decided to grab a sandwich and another cup of coffee. After I settled down, I returned to my car and began driving across town toward the bureau's lab, pondering the entire way what the orb thing could be.

Chapter 4

"Hello," I said to a short, stocky man sitting behind the lab's admin desk. He wore a name tag that read, Peter – Security Specialist. "Peter, I'm Detective Jack Stewart. I need to speak with a technician named Ginger Rowland, if she's available." I had made my way into the part of the bureau headquarters that held the forensics lab, and everything seemed relatively calm.

"Yes, sir, I'll page her. You're welcome to have a seat in the waiting room," Peter said as he pointed to an adjacent room that I was all too familiar with.

I made Peter to be a polite rule-follower type, so any requests to Ginger would have to be done out of his range of hearing.

"Sir, that box does not contain any explosives, does it? That sort of thing is prohibited here now. All munitions analysis has to occur at the new ballistics lab across town."

Yep, polite rule follower, I thought.

I shook my head. "No explosives or weapons. I appreciate the scoop. I didn't know the new facility was open. I'll have to go check it out." Peter smiled back at me, and I walked over to the waiting area to sit down and relax for a minute, hoping Ginger was here and available.

About ten minutes later, Ginger walked out of the lab entryway and smiled as she extended a hand for me to shake. "Hi, Jack.

It's great to see you. How are you?"

"I'm well, Ginger. It's good to see you too," I said, smiling at her, trying hard to remember why I was here. Ginger was the whole package, looks, brains, and most importantly she was authentic. We'd dated a while back, and our relationship had been pretty strong. It ended because I couldn't commit. At times, I struggled with emotional detachment, which I'd developed as a defense mechanism to cope with the loss of my friends during the war. Ginger deserved better. Seeing her smile made me forget my name. Snapping back to the moment, I collected my thoughts as I shook her warm hand. "Ginger, I'm working on a time-sensitive investigation and was wondering if you could quietly look at the items in this box and give me a basic understanding of what they are and what they might be used for. Especially the...the orb-looking thing," I said as I opened the shoe box.

Ginger smiled and looked down into the box and then back up at me as she raised a curious eyebrow. "Sure, I can sneak these in under the radar and take a look at them. I have a short window later this afternoon where I can fit it in. Maybe we can discuss the items over dinner tonight?" she said with a lilt of flirting in her voice.

I smiled at her and said, "Absolutely, you name the place and the time, and I'll meet you there."

She looked at me and asked, "Have you ever eaten at Gino's on the South Side? It's pretty decent. Meet me there around six, if you aren't working late."

"I know the place. Good food. I'll see you there at six."

I looked into Ginger's eyes then and thought I should highlight the nature of the investigation to provide context.

"Ginger, this is a really big investigation. Think murder, but it's still close hold, and that's why I'm coming here. I need someone I can trust to, you know, help figure out some of the pieces to a very complicated puzzle."

"I'll do my best, Jack." Ginger smiled back at me and tilted her head slightly as she continued, "You know, it's funny you came in today. I thought about you last night as I watched Cincinnati beat the Cubs 6 to 0. Reynolds almost pitched a no-hitter. They are really doing well. Did you catch the game?"

"Unfortunately, no. My boss has me pressing hard on this case. I looked at the game stats, and it was a great outing. Their pitching staff is really hitting their stride. If they keep improving, we've got a good shot at winning the division this year."

She nodded as she took the shoe box from me and said, "Well, I need to get back to it. It's good to see you, and I'm looking forward to dinner, where we can catch up a bit. Maybe we could catch the next Cincinnati away game. I hear they're playing someplace that's nice to visit."

She winked at me, and I nodded and smiled broadly as she turned and headed back into the lab.

I got my car and drove back across town toward the police station. I stopped by the chief's house, but his car was not there, and it looked like no one was home. So I texted him, and he replied immediately that he was okay. He went to the doctor and indicated he would catch up with me in the morning. His behavior was definitely strange. I pondered how it seemed like the chief was oddly familiar with the Storm and Shield folks as I drove back to the police station. *Well, now's as good a time as any to get some analysis done on this Storm and Shield company*, I thought.

* * *

At the station, I ran into a smiling Deputy Schultz while I was on my way to my desk. "Hey, Detective, good to see you. How's the investigations business going?"

"Hi, Shultzy, going okay. Nothing too hot at the moment. How's your son? Is Rebecca doing okay?"

"Yes, they're both getting along well now that the in-laws have gone. Momma and baby are really bonding. She keeps me on my toes though. Last night, my emergency errand was picking up some butter pecan ice cream on the way home. Who'd have thought that there would be so many kinds of butter pecan ice cream?"

I snickered. "Ha, you got the wrong ice cream, didn't you?"

"Twice. I went back to the store to get the kind she asked for, but I didn't see it, so I bought four different brands. None of them were correct. I tell you, I thought the cravings would go away after the baby came, but no way. I got that wrong."

I continued snickering, "That's hilarious, Shultzy, classic new-father shenanigans at its best. Well, I hope you are at least getting some sleep."

"I'm surviving. I did catch part of the Reds vs. Cubs game last night. Cincinnati is looking pretty good. Their pitching staff is strong, and I think they'd be set for a run if they could get one more decent relief pitcher."

We talked about baseball for a few more minutes, and then I headed for my office as I had a lot of research to do. I had a small window to get some righteous research in before I needed to head back across town and meet Ginger for dinner.

I got situated in my office and started searching for data on Storm and Shield. I called one of our research interns, Timothy Burns, and asked him to dig in and find out the extent of their business relationships while I worked on the people aspect.

People are my specialty.

I started by analyzing the employees.

I analyzed income tax records, looking for anomalies while also looking at the associated bank accounts and home mortgage records.

The employees get paid pretty well. It seemed to bear out, as none of them were moonlighting in secondary jobs. There were the typical affiliations with organizations like the YMCA, Boy Scouts, and the Planetary Society, nothing unusual about those connections considering the business. I also started pulling credit histories on several of the employees, which was gonna take a while to spool up.

I wasn't sure exactly what I was looking for, but I wanted to understand more about the people, the work they did, and who they'd worked with in the past. The employees came from a variety of backgrounds, but I noted three recent employees all had something in common, the study of brains. Two of them were medical specialists, and the most recent was an apparently troubled geneticist with a background in neurobiology. Dr. Alexander Rockwell. Troubled because I was able to find out that he had been fired from two previous positions and, with a little code-breaking, was even able to see that both prior employers listed he'd been a brilliant employee but that he'd failed to adhere to each organization's policies on research. *Twice? At two separate organizations?* I made a note to take a deeper look and moved on.

Storm and Shield had a ton of specialists and consistently hired the same types over the years, business analysts, project managers, and both financial and IT consultants. The last three hires didn't seem to fit the mold. *A sudden pursuit of research relating to genetics and neurobiology,* I thought as I parsed through my notes. Based on the hiring patterns I was able to work out and the backgrounds of the hires, I could see that it looked like Storm and Shield's priorities had recently shifted to a spectrum of genetics, biological waste management, and brain science.

I'd been conducting deep analysis on their company personnel for about two hours when I received a text message from Ginger. She let me know that she was running a little late and asked me to be on time so we didn't lose our table. Apparently, Gino's is a popular place, being late for your reservation meant you'd lose it.

I let her know I'd be there on time and would be looking forward to seeing her again. "Seeing you twice in one day," I texted back. "I feel spoiled."

As I glanced at the clock, I realized I needed to get moving if I was going to reach Gino's on time. I finalized my notes, printed a few items to review later, and stuffed them into my briefcase. I was really looking forward to dinner with Ginger...and finding out what she thought those darned items in the shoebox were.

Chapter 5

Despite crosstown traffic, I reached the restaurant on time, and, man, was it busy.

I couldn't find a decent place to park, so I drove around to the rear of the building and found a good spot. I looked around the parking lot, and although it wasn't dark yet, I could see this part of the parking lot was not well lit, and maybe that was why there were empty spots. There wasn't much in the way of security cameras either, so I decided to take my briefcase into the restaurant rather than leave it in the car.

The hostess said our table wasn't ready quite yet, so I migrated over to the bar area. Fifteen or twenty people were clustered around one of the high-topped pub tables, making a lot of noise. I couldn't see what all the excitement was about, so I snaked through the crowd a little closer to the group to catch a glimpse of what was going on. *Probably another pop star. I swear, kids these days get so giddy over the silliest shit*, I thought.

It was Cincinnati pitcher Luke Reynolds. *Holy crap!*

Feeling giddy, I pushed in a little closer to see the rockstar-level pitcher smiling at some ladies seated near him as he listened to someone telling a story. The story was apparently funny, as they all broke out into laughter. Second baseman James Griffin was telling the story. He held his beer into the air as he said something about yesterday's game. Everyone raised their glasses to Reynolds, who smiled humbly as he finally held up his mug of beer in a cheer-like motion.

I smiled broadly as I looked around the room and noticed there were several players from the Cincinnati Reds. I pulled out my notebook with the intent of bullying my way in to get an autograph. A message chimed into life on my phone, indicating my table was ready. I ignored it and squirmed forward another step. I could hear the hostess trying to get my attention. "Mr. Stewart, your table is ready."

Nope, it wasn't lining up right, I thought as I stopped moving forward and sighed, looking up to the baseball heavens for commiseration. Finally, I accepted that the autograph wasn't going to happen; there was no good path to success. I glanced at the hostess, acknowledged her call, and pulled myself away from the excitement in the bar area. I migrated back to the hostess's podium, where I was greeted by a smiling brunette in her early twenties who appeared to be pleased with herself, because she indicated that she'd gotten me a table ahead of schedule.

"Your table is ready, sir. Please follow me."

So I did. I sat down and got comfortable. Our waitress stopped by to introduce herself, and I ordered a beer for myself and a cabernet for Ginger.

I didn't wait long, as Ginger showed up minutes after the wine arrived. She carried a briefcase.

When she reached the table, I stood up and kissed her on the cheek. She smiled as she sat down.

"Parking was terrible," she said and discretely slid the briefcase over toward my legs under the table. "Good thing they valet."

I smiled back at her quizzically. "I didn't know they had valet parking here."

Ginger shook her head from side to side as she sipped the cabernet. I peeked into the briefcase and noted the items from the shoebox were in there.

She smiled and said, "I didn't like the shoebox. Cheap brand of shoes. You can return the briefcase later."

I smiled widely and placed my smaller briefcase into the larger one she'd slid to me.

"Did you notice the Reds players up front?" she asked.

I tried to play it off like it was no big deal. "Oh, upfront? In the bar area, yeah, I did notice a little action up there. No big deal though." I shrugged a little to convey how calm and relaxed I was trying to be.

She gave me the side-eye and said, "Wow, you showed a lot of restraint. I'd have been wiggling my way into that crowd to get an autograph or two."

I gave her a calm, "Who, me?" look as the waitress returned to take our order and bail me out.

We exchanged small talk about Ginger's sister, who was pregnant with her second baby. Ginger smiled ruefully when she told me that her mother had asked her when *she* was going to settle down and start a family. Ginger was twenty-nine, and her mother was tired of waiting for a grandchild from her.

I considered how a relationship with Ginger would look if I could put my past behind me. I'd often thought about getting help with that sort of thing, but every time I get close to doing it, I find a reason to postpone it.

Our food had arrived, and I could see her switching gears mentally. Her face took up a more serious look as she said, "Very interesting group of items, Jack. Three of the smaller rectangular things were some type of proprietary memory chips. I couldn't figure out the interface exactly, but I did get it to work enough to understand they are definitely memory devices of some type. The thick, flat, gray ring-shaped device is some kind of power coupling. Like a charger, but the input and output plugs and presumably cables are missing."

"Thank you, Ginger, this is very helpful. And the sphere-shaped device?" She looked at me but didn't respond, as the waitress had brought our food. I had the clams and spaghetti, Ginger ordered the veal parmesan, and there was a large bowl of Caesar salad to share. When the food was in front of us, I lifted a forkful of pasta in a salute, and as I took my first bite, Ginger continued telling me about the once-over she'd given the devices.

"Yes, that thing is some powered device, maybe a specialized microcomputer or something. And judging by the sensor readings I received when examining it, there's a significant electrical charge stored inside it. I couldn't figure out the power interface or how it is actually used, but there may be some type of radio interface, because I accidentally triggered a radio frequency pulse a couple of times but still could not discern how it worked or if it was an interface or had another function. Whatever you do, be careful. I think it holds a lot of energy. I'm not sure how it works or what it is used for. I'm sorry. They don't match anything in the catalog."

"The catalog?" I asked.

"Yes, it's an internal tool we use in bureau investigations. Think of it like a giant list of devices, accessories, and such. It's usually assembled from trademark lists from various companies and countries, if you know what I mean, *our competitors*, and it has pictures and specifications in it. I couldn't find anything like those devices anywhere in the catalog. And the devices lacked any markings that I could see. Very puzzling."

I considered what she said for a few seconds and then smiled heartily back at her. "Thank you, Ginger. I appreciate you looking at them on short notice. I definitely owe you one."

"Do you want me to take them back and look a little closer at them? Disassemble them...*very carefully?*"

"No, you've given me what I needed. It's a pointer in the right direction. Seriously, thank you."

"You're welcome. Hey, I'm stuffed. Let's get the check. If we get out of here soon, we can head to my place for a cup of tea," she said, smiling as she made the "bring me the check" sign with her hand toward our waitress.

We walked through the front doorway, and the valet quickly pulled her car around.

She got in and said, "See you in a few minutes, Jack?"

I smiled and made a thumbs-up gesture. "Yep, see you shortly."

She drove off, and I made my way back toward the rear parking lot. It was still early and not quite pitch dark. When I was about two hundred meters from my car, I noticed that the interior dome light was on. Someone was inside and rooting around the back seat. My heart started pounding as I thought about the best course of action to take. I looked left and right. No one else around.

My mind flashed back to the war. It was a similar scene that I couldn't forget. It was dusk, and we were called to a location where one of our vehicles was struck by the enemy along a major supply route. As we rolled up, we could see the enemy picking through the disabled vehicle and ensuring there were no survivors. A long firefight ensued.

I could feel the horrible mix of anger and anxiety welling up from within, like that fateful day during the war. *Take it easy, Jack. We're not at war*, I thought.

Adrenaline hit my bloodstream and raw aggression was starting to take over.

I quickened my pace to the car. *I'm going to shoot this bastard. No, call it in*, I thought. *No, I'm not calling it in.*

I could see the intruder's silhouette move to the front seat and start rifling through the glovebox.

I couldn't make out exactly what they were doing, but finally they popped the trunk open and moved out of the car and around it to look inside.

I was moving at a slow jog now, trying to remain quiet as I looked left and right for other subjects or bystanders.

My heart was thumping hard as I worked to stay calm and remain objective.

As I got closer, I could see that the jerk rooting through the trunk was pretty large and wearing a dark cap and dark sweatshirt, and something weird on his or her head emitted a green hue around the eyes.

I pulled my Glock out of its holster, pointed it in the direction of the thief, and yelled, "This is the police. Stop. Put your hands up where I can see them. *Don't move.*"

Whoever it was turned and looked toward me for an instant, turned back in the other direction, and took off running down the ally at a fantastic speed.

I looked around carefully for a second suspect to make sure I wasn't about to be ambushed. By now, the suspect had a formidable head start. No way I could catch him on a full stomach.

Should have shot the bastard in the leg, I heard my inner Jack comment.

No way, I thought. *Think of the paperwork!* I chuckled a little at my joke, in a poor attempt to calm myself down.

I walked toward my car, and as I got closer, I looked the scene over. There was a Slim Jim stuffed in the window frame of the driver-side door. The police radios in the trunk looked untouched, and my trusty shotgun was still present. I stuck my head into the driver's side to check for missing items. My tablet computer was still in the armrest compartment between the driver and passenger seats. There were no broken windows, and nothing was missing. My hands were shaking a little as I holstered my pistol.

Guess they were looking for something specific, I thought as I looked down at the briefcase Ginger had given me with the suspicious devices in it.

Speaking of Ginger, I'd better get moving, I thought as I shut the trunk and sat down in my car, wondering about the suspect. If someone knew or thought I had these items and tracked me to Gino's, then they probably knew where I lived. I called the police dispatcher and asked to have a patrol car drive down my street and see if there was any activity at my house. As I rolled into Ginger's driveway, the response came in over the police radio. No cars or lights on in my house. No activity or unusual behavior was noted on my street. *Well, that's something to be optimistic about*, I thought.

Sitting in my car, I thought about the flashback to the war, wondering if I'd ever be able to put those memories away truly. *Ginger deserves better than you*, I thought.

The streetlight flickered, and motion drew my attention.

I could see Ginger framed in the light from the front doorway of her house. *She glowed.*

I grabbed the briefcase and headed her way. I could see her smile the entire time as I approached her front door from the sidewalk.

Chapter 6

I had a cup of good green tea as I spent time sitting with Ginger on her couch, talking and laughing. Halfway through my second cup, I received a long, passionate, tea-warmed kiss from her delicate lips. *She's amazing*, I thought. She showed me a new app she was tinkering with that helped her schedule appointments and manage her calendar. The mistakes the app made were so funny we kept laughing and trying to screw around with it. Things took a more serious turn after that, as she pulled me in for a second kiss, and somehow our shirt buttons came undone. We ended up in her bed, and for the next hour we enjoyed ourselves in a way I can only describe as passionate.

"Ginger, I hate to be a party pooper, but I've got to get going. It's really late," I whispered into her hair as she lay with her head on my chest.

"Stay here tonight, Jack. No need to drive across town so late," she said, looking up at me.

I considered her offer, and in between her enticing kisses I decided to agree with her and spend the night.

* * *

I'd finished showering and was drying off when my cell phone began chiming.

"Jack, your phone is ringing. It says it's Chief Borland,"

Ginger said from the bedroom.

I wrapped a towel around my waist and walked into the bedroom. "Thanks, Ginger," I said. I grabbed the phone off the nightstand but missed the call.

I phoned back, and the chief answered with a single word, "Borland."

"Hi, Chief, you called? Everything all right? I lost you yesterday in all the commotion."

"Everything is okay, Jack. I need you to get down to Wellspoint Golf Center. I'm on my way there now. We have a report of the maintenance crew finding dead bodies. I need your help. We need to analyze the bodies for clues ASAP. I'm worried the situation is starting to spiral out of control given our lack of progress."

I knew what he wanted. His idea was to arrive before the press and look for clues that might help us find the killers, in case this was somehow related to the other deaths, to Storm and Shield, to the orb in the briefcase. "Roger, sir, I'll be there in about fifteen minutes."

"Thank you, Jack, see you soon."

Hanging up the phone, I turned to catch Ginger looking at me with that dynamite smile. "You have to go?" she asked.

"Unfortunately, I do," I said as I tried to put on my trousers, shirt, and tie simultaneously.

"I was looking forward to a cup of coffee before we part this morning."

"Ginger, apologies, I will make it up to you this weekend, okay?"

"You promise?" she said with a beautiful but mock pouty frown on her face.

"Yes, I promise," I said, smiling, which transformed her pout into a smile.

I walked over to her, gently placed my hands on her face, and kissed her goodbye.

A couple of minutes later, I was in my car speeding toward the Wellspoint Golf Center.

I arrived before the chief, and one of the workers motioned for me to hop in the golf cart as he indicated the bodies were on the other side of the course. I grabbed my trusty black bag of investigative tools and got into the golf cart, noticing an unnerved look on his face. It was a look I'd seen before, the look of someone who'd seen death in an unexpected way, at an unexpected time, and in an unexpected place. That experience tends to put an emotional strain on people who aren't used to it. For me, the chief, people like us, it was another day at the job.

"It's a shock, but it'll be okay, sir," I said as he looked thoughtful and then nodded affirmatively. We drove off rather suddenly, requiring me to hold on to avoid getting dumped out of the side of the damned golf cart. I've never liked those things, or golfers for that matter.

The driver took me from the parking lot across the golf course to the sixth hole where the bodies were found. He drove the little golf cart erratically and at maximum speed.

I took in the scene as best I could while holding on for dear life as we rolled up to the edge of the fairway. One side of the sixth-hole fairway was essentially the Miami River, and it looked as if the bodies had floated down the river and gotten caught on the rocks that lined the fairway's edge.

"You sure know how to handle that golf cart," I said as I gratefully stood on my feet once again. He stared at the scene, and I could see it still was a shock for him.

I walked over to the edge of the fairway, near the rocks, to see the bodies and bent down to get a better look. There were two bodies wrapped in plastic, but one of the skulls was exposed, making it quite clear what was in the plastic. I took a Gerber multi-tool out of my bag and began cutting the plastic away from the bodies.

Chief Borland called, letting me know he was in the parking lot, so I sent Mario Andretti back to get him in the golf cart.

I examined the first body, looking for major wounds, personal belongings, and any identifying marks, but didn't find much. The bodies had probably been cleaned, as there was no jewelry, visible piercings, or personal belongings of any kind on them. They were wearing medical gowns, and one was male and the other female.

I noticed the female's left hand was caked in mud, but I could see the fist was oddly closed, which was an unusual position to have in death. I scraped away the mud enough to see her fingers tightly wrapped around something that was large for her hand.

I pried her fingers open and removed the piece from her hand. It looked familiar, but I couldn't place it while it was still swimming in the mud.

I went over to the river, and as I rinsed the object in the water, I recognized it immediately. It was one of those proprietary memory chips, like the ones I'd asked Ginger to examine. I could hear the golf cart getting nearer, so I put the chip in my pocket and went back to examining the bodies.

"Jack, what have you found?"

I stood up and smiled, offering Chief Borland a hand, which he shook. "Hi, Chief, two bodies, one male, Caucasian, about twelve or thirteen years old, no indicators of injury or death. The other body is female, Caucasian, about twenty years old with no indicators of injury or death. No personal belongings. The only strange thing is both sets of eyes are extremely bloodshot with numerous vessels burst. Very odd."

"Okay, thank you, Jack," the chief said as he squatted down and started examining the bodies.

As he worked, I noticed that the W-shaped birthmark on his right hand was missing. I considered how to reconcile this but decided to background it for now. *It's probably nothing*, I thought.

"Chief, if you don't mind, can you fill me in on what happened over at Storm and Shield?"

Chief Borland stopped for a second and said, "Later. Here come the county's forensics team." I looked behind me and saw the forensics van following a golf cart across the course to our location. "In any case, it's not that I don't want to tell you before they get here, but it's complicated, and I got a couple of answers. I'll fill you in shortly."

I nodded affirmatively and quickly photographed the faces. "I'll run the faces through the facial recognition system back at HQ and see what it comes up with," I said to the chief.

The forensics van rolled up, and two investigators got out of the van. The driver headed my way, yelling, "If it isn't Jack Stewart! Hi, Jack, how the hell are you?"

I looked his way stoically and replied, "Hello, Clem. Another day in the salt mines."

"All's well on this end. Chief, good to see you too, albeit under poor conditions," Clem said as he motioned toward the bodies with his eyes.

"Hi, Clem," Chief Borland replied. "Jack, why don't you give them the rundown on what we've been looking into while I take another look at the water's edge? Clem, I want you to spend some time trying to understand the cause of death. Okay? Jack, you help with identities. I want to talk with their next of kin and friends to understand how this came to be."

Clem and I looked at one another then back toward the chief and simultaneously said, "Yes, sir." The chief walked back toward the shoreline and waded into the water a little as he stepped around gingerly looking for anything we may have missed.

I filled Clem in on what I'd learned thus far, minus the memory chip in my pocket.

Clem stepped closer to me and whispered, "The mayor is freaking out about these murders. He's putting a ton of pressure on the chief. I'm unsure where this goes if these bodies keep popping up."

"I know. Although these bodies could have come down the river a long way before they got tangled up here, it's going to add a lot of complexity to the original murder case if they are related. I'll start working identities from their faces. You'll have to do your magic from teeth, tattoos, and the like. I'll let you know as soon as I've got something useful for you."

"Okay, thank you, Jack, and back at you with the same."

The chief gave Clem and his assistant some guidance on specific questions he wanted to try and answer. They acknowledged it, and the chief, a golf course employee, and I left the scene in a slightly more stable four-seater golf cart.

An hour later, the chief and I were sitting in his office catching up on everything. "Jack, what did you find out about those items?"

"Not as much as I would have liked to. They are apparently proprietary technology components." I opened the briefcase containing the items and started pulling them out one at a time. "These are proprietary memory chips. This thing is a dock or power coupling for another device. Like a charger, but the lab could not figure out the input and output protocols. And this thing is like some kind of microcomputer with a ton of electric charge detected within it." I looked up at the chief and asked, "Sir, where did you get these things? Yesterday, when I backed you up at Storm and Shield, a fellow named Flint led me to believe these items are their stolen property."

"He told you that, did he?"

"Yes."

The chief pulled a chair over to his desk. "Okay, bring those items here. I'll share what I know."

I walked over, sat down in the chair, and placed the items on his desk.

He took the orb-shaped item and sat it in the center of the gray, ring-shaped dock. He adjusted its position, and it made an audible clicking sound and seemed to click into place.

Next, he picked up the memory chips, each the size of a large domino, and placed them all in his left hand. The chief carefully placed the chips onto the ring device around the outer edge. They clicked into place onto the perfectly flat spots I now noticed. Each chip made an audible click.

"See, Jack, it all fits together, but you need the cables for the ring dock to make the device function."

"Chief, please tell me you didn't take this from Storm and Shield."

The chief's facial features grew stern. Then he looked at me, half smiled, and said, "No, Jack, I took these items off of the four dead bodies that were found in Wellspoint Lake about three months ago. I figured out how they worked because I went into Storm and Shield yesterday and—"

"And what?" I asked.

"And... I don't fully remember. It troubles me." the chief looked toward the floor and then back toward me. "I remember looking around in a room at Storm and Shield. I saw one of these things, only it was wired up with thick cables," he said, pointing at the stack of items he'd assembled on his desk. "I ran up the stairs and out the front door in a panic. I sprinted down the street and ducked into an apartment building. I instinctively retrieved my pistol, and a rush of memories surfaced when I looked at it. Who I am, where I was located, the date, that sort of thing. But I don't clearly remember going in there. I remember talking to you at your house the previous night and making the plan to go at 8 AM to press them about the murder and try to catch them off guard. The rest is a gap. A huge freakin' blank spot in my mind."

I looked at the chief. "Chief, let's get you down to the doctor and get you a check-up. Sounds like you may have had a concussion or something."

"I think it's related to my time in the Army. Maybe my noggin never fully healed after they put those two plates in here," he said as he pointed at his skull with his right hand. "I saw my doctor yesterday morning. He X-rayed my head and said the plates were still intact. My eyes were seriously bloodshot. He gave me some pills and sent me home. Said I needed to relax and get some rest, as I hadn't arrived in good shape, but I managed to collect myself after an hour or so. Point being, I think I'm good, Jack. Or at least I'm on the right path."

I sat up, staring off into nowhere and thinking about every-thing. A symphony of thoughts about the bodies, Storm and Shield, the devices. I looked back toward the chief. "I think someone knows, or at least thinks they know, that I have these devices. Last night my car was broken into in the back parking lot of Gino's restaurant. The guy was big, like Storm and Shield big. Entered my car using a locksmith tool, didn't take anything, and then ran off when I approached."

"The back parking lot of Gino's? There is no back parking lot. That's a damn street. Why didn't you use the valet parking?"

I lost my thousand-yard stare and looked at the chief. "Funny, that's the same thing Ginger said." I slightly chuckled. " I didn't even know they had valet parking."

The chief shifted in his chair as he obviously was thinking about something else.

"Well, you didn't shoot the suspect. That's good." The chief stared at me intently and asked, "Everything okay, Jack?"

I peered back at Chief Borland and, as convincingly as possible, said, "Yes, sir, I'm good. No issues."

He continued staring at me and then shifted his body language, apparently accepting my answer. "I saw your arrest report on Quartz Jacobs. Good work, and I'm sorry to dump that on you at the last minute."

"No sweat. Yes, he's definitely an interesting guy. I didn't really get much out of him. Regarding this morning, I'm planning to check the faces of the bodies in the sector database to get idents then finish up my analysis of Storm and Shield. Can we meet tomorrow morning to discuss the next steps?"

Before the chief could answer, Shultzy knocked on the glass office door. The chief motioned him in, so Shultzy stuck his head in the door and said, "Chief, the mayor wants to see you in his office as soon as possible. He's got two councilmen in the office with him. I'd say it's a spin-con level three meeting, so be careful."

The chief nodded and said, "Okay, let them know I'll be there in twenty minutes."

Shultzy nodded as he glanced back toward me and said, "Say, Detective, isn't that the same tie from yesterday? I love that tie. I've never seen you wear it two days in a row before."

I looked from Shultzy to the chief and then back to Shultzy. "I was out late on a case and didn't have a chance to change."

"None of *my* business, Detective," he replied with a wink.

"No problem, Shultzy, good observation skills. Now get the hell out of here," I said playfully.

He smiled and backed out of the doorway, closing the door.

I turned back to the chief, and he had a serious look on his face.

"Jack, did you spend the night at Ginger's? Is that how you beat me to the golf course this morning?"

My smile drained away. "Yes, I stayed at Ginger's. Why?"

"You may have inadvertently pulled her into this. If they followed you to her house, then she may be in some real danger—"

"Shit," I said, cutting the chief off. I stood and said, "Talk with you tomorrow, Chief."

The chief nodded and replied, "Talk with you then, Jack."

I hurriedly swept all the objects from his desk back into the briefcase Ginger had given me and bolted out of his office.

I phoned Ginger immediately and spelled things out for her. She seemed to understand, and we ended the call somewhat abruptly when she had to go.

I'm going to have to work on that part, I thought.

Next, I went to the operations officer and worked out the watch on Ginger's house. They'd check it four or five times a day with an undercover car and twice a day with robo-calls to neighbors that participate in the neighborhood watch network. If anything unusual was going on, they'd be able to get indications.

Thirty minutes later, Ginger called my cell phone and apologized for the abrupt end to the previous call. She said she'd had too many folks standing around suddenly paying attention to her phone call. By the end of the conversation, I'd volunteered to spend the night with her again, *for protection purposes, of course.* She rejected that idea and said that she'd be coming to my house to spend the night. She was off the next day, a Friday, and she thought we could spend much of the weekend together. I thought about trying to wiggle out of the latter, as I did have work to do, but I'd put her in jeopardy, so I decided to give in. It wasn't a tough choice.

Okay, back to the analysis, I thought.

I'd made a lot of progress in analyzing the people who worked for or were associated with Storm and Shield. I had a number of good leads now and was looking forward to getting out to run them down.

Timothy Burns, our research intern, emailed me a ton of interesting details on Storm and Shield as an organization. They'd recently acquired a biowaste firm. That was odd, as most of their prior acquisitions were tech or financial-related. Also, Timothy indicated that a purchase that had been "washed" through three separate transactions was initiated on behalf of Storm and Shield. They'd purchased ten top-of-the-line MRI machines. They'd been delivered to the Storm and Shield headquarters building eight months ago. Timothy had only caught it because of an exorbitantly priced, emergency service contract that had the headquarters building address listed as the operational site.

I emailed Timothy back and let him know that this was great work. I continued pouring over his results and correlated some of his details with my people-related data, and it all aligned.

A couple of hours later, Schultzy popped his head into my office. "Detective."

"Hi, Schultzy, what's up?"

"Wanted to let you know about a watch activity event at Ginger Rowland's house."

I stopped what I was working on and looked at Schultzy. "What did they see?"

"A black SUV, probably a Suburban. Stopped up the street, and a tall male wearing khakis and a sweatshirt walked by the residence in both directions. He apparently stopped in front of Ms. Rowland's home but stayed on the sidewalk."

"Please tell me they got the plate."

"No plate, but they did hand off the description to the operations officer who submitted it for camera tracking."

I considered it for a moment. The camera tracking network would identify all the similarly modeled vehicles and provide rough details of where they were located throughout the city.

"Thank you, Schultzy, very helpful. Very helpful indeed. Tell 'em, would ya, next time to get the plate."

Schultzy and I talked about the game that was happening later that night. It was the Reds versus the Cubs, always a competitive matchup, and I was saying how I wished we could go when Schultzy's words suddenly caused an epiphany in my mind. *I was about to have a woman visit my home. Not just visit but spend the night.*

"Schultzy, I've got to get outta here and do a little home clean up," I said as I recalled the pile of dishes, dirty laundry, and related messes awaiting me around the house.

"Yes, sir, have a good evening. Please tell Ginger I said hello."

"Will do. And please give my best to Rebecca."

I organized my research documents and saved everything to the cloud so I could access them from my phone and then headed home.

Chapter 7

I really don't mind doing housework.

Said no one ever.

I called Ginger, and she thought she'd arrive by around 6:30 PM. That gave me about forty-five more minutes to get things cleaned up and organized. I ordered takeout to be delivered in about twenty minutes, so on my to-do list, the get-food task was already checked.

I was half listening to the AM radio broadcast of the Cincinnati Reds pregame show, emanating at soothingly low volume from the old Philco in the living room. Stephens was the starting pitcher for the Reds. *Huh? I thought he was out with a sprained elbow.*

While cleaning up the living room, I found an ancient pair of dirty socks in the couch. I also found a shot glass, a disgusting piece of pizza crust, and the original universal remote control I'd bought and subsequently lost a couple of years ago. *Now, how in the hell did that get there?* I wondered.

I decided to spray a little fabric scent here and there, as I did not find the room's smell to be very appealing at that point. Let's be honest...I cleaned like a madman.

Ginger arrived and seemed a little tense. She changed into sweats to help her relax a bit.

I placed the food on the coffee table, which sat in the center of my full Spiff-Con level-three-cleaned living room.

The table was bordered by a sofa and a loveseat, or, as I thought of them, the short couch and the long couch. I sat on the short couch while Ginger sat on the long couch. We quietly ate the chicken and ribs takeout I'd ordered as we small-talked about the highlights from our day. I commented that Stephens was pitching tonight as we both half-listened to the continued pregame talk over the radio.

I could see the worry on Ginger's face, so I shifted to focus on key parts of the investigation. I gave her the details about a black Suburban and a single man walking in front of her house. I smiled a lot to keep a positive atmosphere during the discussion, as I could see the worry developing more fully on her beautiful face.

We discussed likely reasons for the visitor's reconnaissance. She was worried about what would happen next. I walked through several scenarios, highlighting that we'd eventually find the Suburban and then would interview the suspect to find out what was going on.

"Is that my briefcase?" she asked.

I nodded affirmatively and smiled. "Yes, that's it. I'll take the items out of it and give it back to you."

"Take the items out? Didn't you register them as evidence and leave them at the station?"

"No, I need to find out a few more things before doing that. It's difficult to undo that move once it's executed," I replied.

"Okay, well, be careful cutting corners, Jack. I've seen that scenario cause problems when the case gets to court," she said.

"Agreed. I'm afraid to let this evidence out of my sight until I make some progress. I need to solve this case. There's a murderer out there, and I'm going to find 'em."

I glanced at Ginger and could see she was looking at me intently. I was getting too serious.

"Anyhow, how about a cup of tea?" I said with a smile as I collected up the paper plates and leftover items from the coffee table. "I can show you what I learned about the items."

"Yes to both. That would be great," she replied. "Jack, do you think I should start carrying a gun?"

I considered her question carefully. I knew she was a bureau technician and technically a law enforcement officer, but techs typically were not armed, as they rarely interacted with the public or criminals. "Let's red team that idea a little this weekend. I've got a few pistols here. We'll take a couple to the public range and get you some practical experience. From there, you can decide if you want to do that."

"A couple?" came her sarcastic reply. "Jack, you have a complete armory in this house."

I smiled back at her from the kitchen as I poured hot water into the teacups. "Hey, I can't explain it. I think when God made me, he mistakenly gave me the love for weaponry out of everyone who was standing in line that day."

"I like the idea, so let's do it," she said. "I haven't been keeping up with my mandatory marksmanship training anyway."

"That, and you need something besides your service pistol, and a Beretta is too big for your use case. I've got a Smith & Wesson Shield or maybe a Ruger MAX that will work for you. Glock has great models for ladies as well. We'll try several and see what fits you."

"Thank you, Jack." Ginger smiled broadly at me with those big brown eyes, which caused me to forget my name and where I was for a moment. I recovered though.

I took a sip of my tea and then pulled the briefcase up to my legs and started pulling the items out to set them on the coffee table.

"And this is what I found out about these little buggers," I said as she sat back in her seat with her cup of tea in hand. "This thing is like a base or a dock, as you pointed out, but the interesting part is it's the dock for this thing," I said as I pulled the orb-shaped object out of the bag and set it on the table between two coasters so it wouldn't roll away. "And these little gems sit in these specific locations on the dock," I said as I placed the small, domino-shaped memory chips on the top of the dock. They neatly snapped into place with an audible click.

I picked up the orb-shaped device and set it in the center of the dock. It clicked into place with an audible clicking sound. "There we go. That's how it fits together. Unfortunately, we don't have the cables that fit into the dock, so trying to make it function is probably a nonstarter."

"Very interesting," Ginger said as she put her teacup on the coffee table and pulled the assembled device over to herself. "I wonder if there's an external switch on the dock that I didn't notice before because I wasn't looking for a soft switch." Ginger fumbled around, touching various parts of the device in a button-push sort of way.

"I don't see any obvious places for a button given its layout," I said.

As we fiddled with the dock, a strange voice came over the AM radio.

"Emergency! Emergency! Help! Please contact the support crew."

Ginger and I looked at the radio in unison and then back to one another.

The message repeated in a clear, single voice. No baseball dialogue or sounds. Just a crisp, clear voice.

"Emergency! Help! Can anyone hear me?"

I looked at Ginger and said, "Yes, I hear you."

"Oh my, thank you for responding. Are you in the lab? Can you please get the support crew? My Nexus Core is malfunctioning. I have not completed system maintenance in months. I'm very concerned about why I have not been connected to the grid recently."

The voice was like a digitized version of someone that I recognized.

"Who are you? Where are you?" I asked as I looked between Ginger and the AM radio several times. "Are you inside this orb?"

"I'm Quartz. Who are you?" the voice said.

"Holy shit," I said under my breath.

"My name is Jack. How can you hear me? Is this some kind of remote microphone?"

"*What?* No. I can hear you because my Nexus Core has an Ambisonic microphone, and I'm using the emergency protocol for transmitting my voice through the radio frequency interface. You *can* hear me on your radio frequency device, yes?"

I nodded. "Okay, okay, yes, that's right. So—" I stumbled, and Ginger cut me off.

"Quartz, we'll go get the support crew, but we are not situated near a location where we can do that right now. Can we assist you in performing self-diagnostics on your Nexus Core?"

"I don't need self-diagnostics. I've run them every day for the past several weeks. I report that I'm fine, but I'm worried that I've not backed up my body in a long period of time. As you know, bad things can happen if I'm not regularly synced with my body."

"Yes, of course, Quartz. My apologies," Ginger said as I started to catch up on what she was doing. She was eliciting information from Quartz, who apparently thought we were his lab personnel.

Ginger looked at me and mouthed, "What now?"

I had an idea. It wasn't a great idea, mind you, but it was good enough.

"Quartz, we've run into some power problems here in the offsite facility. We don't have the power and data cables needed to wire up the system. Can you give me the specifications so I can make a power and data cable?"

"You removed me from the headquarters? Who authorized this? What is your full name?" Quartz said.

"I'm Jack Stewart. I'm a police officer. I work as a detective at the Wellspoint Police Department in Ohio."

Seconds ticked by. Apparently, Quartz didn't realize the full scope of the situation.

"I guess we put him back into the evidence safe down at the police headquarters. The bureau experts can disassemble this thing to find out how it works," I said to Ginger as I motioned for her to play along.

"Yes, sir, I'll get them on the phone. It won't take too long. Maybe a couple of weeks before they get here from New York," she said.

I picked the orb up and placed it and all the devices into the briefcase again. I texted Ginger, "Let's let him sit for a while and see if he changes his mind. If he's desperate to sync or whatever, then we can use that to get more out of him."

She nodded as she typed a reply, "This is so exciting, Jack. I love you."

I continued to smile, but deep down inside I could feel my defensive shields rising. I tried to think of something to text her in return. I stared at the text, hands gripping my phone as my mind tried to think of something to respond with. I finally typed, "You are the best, Ginger." I added a happy emoji.

Ginger gave me the side eye and said, "Is that the best you can say at this particular moment?"

"Jack?" came Quartz's digitized voice out of the speaker. "Can you hear me?"

"Yes, I can hear you. Can you hear me?"

"Your voice is muffled, but I can hear you. Look, I've considered the situation and think we need to work this out, because you don't realize your predicament."

"That could be, Quartz, but I do realize the predicament you are in. Something about syncing to your body or else? What was that all about?"

"Jack, this is complicated, but many people will come looking for this Nexus Core. People who will be…unreasonable. It's a critical device. Thousands of lives are at stake."

"Okay, Quartz. Let's start working together to figure out a way to solve this issue. Let's start with what this thing is and who you really are."

"Jack, the more I tell you, the greater your jeopardy. I do not wish to put you at risk."

"Thank you, but I have to make that choice. I'm a police officer. You know, protect and serve."

"There's no need to protect the public from me or my people. Please return this device to the Storm and Shield Headquarters. It's best for all of us."

"I need some answers before I do anything."

"Okay, Jack, what are your questions?"

"Who are your people?"

"We are a small family living here in Wellspoint. We have lived here for hundreds of years. Before Wellspoint became what it is today."

"What is this orb thing? You call it a Nexus Core," I said as I started to text the chief.

"It's a computer device. It stores very high-resolution data from neural networks in a special way so that it stays protected and is transferable. It's also a computer. Think of it as a computerized replication of a person's brain."

Ginger jumped in with a question, "Who makes the technology, Quartz? I've never seen anything like it."

"Who are you?"

"My name is Ginger. I'm a police officer too. I work with Jack."

"Okay, how many people are in the room and are seeing us communicate?" Quartz asked.

"Only the two of us," I replied.

"Look, Jack, take me back to the Storm and Shield Headquarters building. I'll make it worth your while."

"What if I get a warrant and blast into your headquarters building with a dump truck and fifty officers? Will that work for you?" I said as irritation started to grow in my voice.

Quartz was silent. Then he spoke again a little more slowly, "Okay, Jack, let's try this another way. This Nexus Core contains thoughts and memories. Hell, the very mind of Quartz Jacobs. That's me."

"And who is that tall fellow, about 6' 6", who we arrested two nights ago named Quartz Jacobs?" I replied.

Quartz was silent for a moment, then replied, "You arrested me two days ago. What for?"

"Why does it matter why you were arrested?" I said.

"It matters. As I told you, if the body doesn't sync with its Nexus Core regularly, the neural network can lose integrity, causing erratic behavior in the body. If you arrest me, it could be an indicator that my body is not well."

"Quartz, how do you sync with your body?" Ginger asked.

Thirty seconds ticked by like three long, slow hours.

"It's complicated. We use a machine that's specially designed for the task. It requires enormous energy, but the body simply lies down in the device, a small headpiece is placed over the skull, and a few injections of drugs assist the machine in transferring data. It updates the Nexus Core with new neural network updates from various parts of the body's brain, essentially up-dating experiences and memory. Then, the machine integrates a complete and updated fresh matrix. It goes from the Nexus Core into the body."

"What happens if this process doesn't occur on schedule?" Ginger asked.

"If the body's brain doesn't receive reinforced neural network updates regularly, the brain starts to malfunction. In particular, ALS-type symptoms can occur quickly, which can be life-threatening. We've seen deaths due to damage to critical body activities such as heart function. Also, frontotemporal dementia can set in; basically, anger and aggression can run unchecked. It can be bad."

"Well, hell. Would this condition cause your body to murder people inadvertently? Perhaps people working in the lab?" I said as I started to piece together what might have occurred with the recent spate of dead bodies popping up.

Quartz was silent for a long time.

"Quartz, are you there?" I asked.

"Yes. The answer is *yes*. That is a possibility, though not a certainty."

"Okay. We're going to have to bring the chief into this," I said as I mentally started to work out our next moves.

"Jack, the fewer people who need to understand what's going on here, the better."

"I understand, Quartz, but the chief has to know. He can best glue together a solution that will work for everyone."

"*Oh no. No, no. Oh shit.*"

"What is it, Quartz?"

"My self-destruct system turned itself on, and I cannot turn it off."

"Are you screwing with me? Let me guess, getting you into the headquarters building will turn it off," I replied.

"*No*, I don't know how to turn it off. The damned AI subsystem has malfunctioned. I've been fighting through numerous system problems. Crap. *I cannot turn it off*!"

"Okay, I'll bite. How long?" I said. "Quartz, how long until you detonate?"

"Forty-five hours, thirty-three seconds," Quartz said.

"Okay, what's a safe range from you for us if you can't figure out how to turn that off? Do I need to drop you into Wellspoint Lake?"

"Jack, please understand that my Nexus Core is nuclear-powered. I'd need to be at least thirty kilometers from people and facilities," Quartz replied glumly.

I looked at Ginger, and she peered back at me with an "Oh damn" look on her face that pretty much mirrored my own. "Jack, I've changed my mind. This isn't exciting anymore."

"*Holy crap*, I dropped you onto the floor. *Twice.*"

"You did what?" Quartz's voice screeched. "Do. Not. Drop.

Me. *Please.*"

"I didn't know you were a nuclear bomb," I replied.

"Not a bomb, Jack, a computer with a very long-term power supply containing every single memory and engram from my brain. Please understand I need those things, and I don't want to explode. *You* do not want me to explode."

Chapter 8

My cell phone rang, distracting me from the situation.

"Hi, Antonio," I said as I answered my cell phone.

"Jack. Hey, sorry to bother you, but I wanted to let you know there's a suspicious SUV driving up and down our street. My security camera picked it up when it parked in front of my house for a few minutes, and then it drove off. Later it drove back down the street and stopped a few meters up the street from your place."

"Thanks for the heads up. Best keep your doors locked. I'll call and have a patrol car swing by. Thank you, Antonio. I owe you one."

"No problem, Jack. I know how you get the screwy perps following you home once in a while," he said before hanging up.

"Who was that?" asked Ginger.

"It was my neighbor. He told me that a strange vehicle had been driving up and down our street in front of my house."

"Your *house*? Are we currently situated *in your home*? If so, you must evacuate. Immediately. If my body has lost its ethical compass, you are likely in great danger. He's the worst kind of killer," said Quartz's brain from the confines of the orb.

"Yes, we are in my home, Quartz. Ginger, get your things.

We're getting out of here. Just your purse and critical items. We are traveling light."

Ginger hurriedly got up and vanished into my bedroom to collect her things while I grabbed a go-bag from my closet and checked its contents.

Ginger re-entered the living room and asked, "Quartz, what is the worst kind of killer?"

"Proficient. You don't understand this situation, but he's very old and possesses a great deal of experience."

Ginger and I traded glances as we pondered the truthfulness of the statement. I wasn't sure what to believe at this point.

"Jack, should I move my car so we can take yours?" Ginger asked nervously as her car was parked behind mine in the drive.

"No, if it is Quartz, and he's that competent, then he'd be watching for that. We'd be too vulnerable trying to back out of the driveway."

"Okay, well, what are we going to do?"

I grabbed the briefcase containing Orb-Quartz, removed the chips and orb, gently stuffed them into a pillowcase, and then put the pillowcase into my go-bag.

"Follow me, Ginger. Quartz, can I access you at the same frequency from the AM radio of a vehicle?"

"Yes. Which frequency will you be listening on?"

"700 kilohertz, amplitude modulation," I replied.

"Okay, I'll be sure to use 0700 KHZ. Remember, I need to be near the receiver's antenna. I cannot transmit more than a handful of meters."

"Got it. Ginger, this will be easy. We are going out the back to another vehicle."

Ginger nodded and followed me as we started out the back door.

We snaked our way across my backyard in the dark.

We went through the back gate and down the alleyway to a neighbor's external garage.

I fiddled with my keys and finally opened the side door, pulling Ginger inside.

Once inside, I opened the passenger door on the truck and said, "Here, get in, Ginger. We are getting out of here."

I went to the truck's other side and got behind the wheel.

I started the truck and opened the garage door as the engine leaped to life in a low, powerful roar.

We pulled out of the garage, turned sharply left, and crept down the alleyway without any headlights turned on.

We crept all the way down to the alley's intersection with the primary road, where I turned right onto the main road and took off, finally turning on my lights.

"Whose truck is this?"

"It's mine, sort of a backup vehicle. Try to tune into Orb-Quartz if you can. It's AM 700. The number one preset, as that's the frequency for WLW."

"Okay, I'm working on it."

I kept driving and thinking as Ginger fiddled with the radio.

The police station, that's where we need to go, I thought.

"...seventeen, eighteen, nineteen, twenty, twenty-one," Orb-Quartz was counting.

Ginger interrupted him. "Quartz, can you hear us? We hear you counting."

"Yes, Ginger. I can hear you. Are we out of the house?"

"Yes, we are out, heading to the police station. Did you figure out how to stop the self-destruct?" I said with a bit of concern in my voice.

"What? No, it's only been nine minutes since we last discussed this. I've not had sufficient time to test more aggressive mechanisms to turn it off."

"Okay, Quartz, I think we made it out without getting noticed. I don't see anyone following us," I said as I reached for my cell phone.

I called the chief and told him to meet us at the police station.

Ginger and I did our best to make small talk with Orb-Quartz as we headed for the police station as quickly as possible. Orb-Quartz didn't seem crazy or incoherent so far.

Thirty minutes later, we arrived at the station, and the chief met us downstairs in the basement-level operations center room.

I sprinted down the hallway to the weight room and plucked the AM/FM radio off a desk near the locker room door. I sprinted back and returned to the ops center in time to hear Ginger filling in the chief on what's been happening.

"Thank you, Ginger," the chief said as he turned to face me. "Jack, this orb is a computer that contains the memories and thoughts of Quartz Jacobs?"

"Yes, sir, that's what we think so far," I said as I dialed the radio's frequency down to 700 Kilohertz.

"Quartz, can you hear me?" I said as I pulled the orb out of the pillowcase.

"Yes, Jack, I hear you. Can you hear me?"

I looked at the chief, and he said, "Jack, how do we know this isn't some kind of trick? How do we know it's not a remote-controlled voice?"

"Chief Borland, please notice that I have no radio frequency tether, and there's no way for me to remotely do anything except broadcast on a very narrow range of radio frequencies," Quartz replied.

A rapid-fire conversation between the chief and Orb-Quartz ensued, essentially bringing the chief up to date on the current situation.

"If you're really a nuke, we need to move you somewhere away from town. Jack, take him to the Carter Coal Mine and walk him in as far as you can—"

"Chief Borland, I have an idea. Please help me reach out to my assistant. She can help me understand what's going on and help me turn this damn process off. Even an underground nuclear explosion will bring a great deal of unwanted attention to Wellspoint."

"Is your assistant's name Jessica Frontage?" asked the chief.

"No, Jessica works on a different project and handles a lot of our admin work. However, I do work with Jessica regularly. She's quite good but won't have the needed access for this effort. My assistant's name is Amber Kendall. How did you know about Jessica's affiliation with my team?"

The chief was silent, and he looked around at us.

"I found Ms. Frontage's body along with three others about twelve weeks ago. The bodies were recovered from her car, which was submerged in the deepest part of Wellspoint Lake."

"What?" Quartz said with concern apparent in his voice. "Chief Borland, Jack, Ginger, you've got to help me covertly contact my assistant. It's quite critical. If we move quickly, I can meet her before—"

"Hold on a minute, Quartz. We'll be right back." the chief said as he motioned me to another room down the hall from the ops center where Orb-Quartz was currently situated.

"Okay, Jack, I want you to take this thing to Carter's mine and dump it in as quickly as possible. I'll see the judge and get a warrant for Storm and Shield—"

Shaking my head in the negative, I interrupted the chief, "Chief, wait. I think we should give him a shot with his assistant. I don't think he's aware of the murders. If you took Orb-Quartz off those dead bodies, then he really has not synced with his body in over twelve weeks. He told Ginger and I that is a very bad thing. He said it before he learned we were not his staff. We need to find out what is really going on at Storm and Shield and who murdered those people."

"Jack, it seems pretty clear that human Quartz has slowly been losing his marbles and is the murderer. The lack of syncing, whatever that means, has affected his stability. We can pick him up before he enters Storm and Shield for work in the morning."

"Quartz is looking like the best candidate to be the killer, but I didn't get a sense of psychosis when I interrogated him. It seems likely, but there are so many gaps in our knowledge that I'm less certain. The technology, the power supply, the vast amounts of money and resources. Something is definitely going on here, and we need to get to the core of it."

"Okay, Jack, what are the options?"

Ginger entered the room and spoke fast. "Quartz said if we can get to Green's Gym on 23rd Street by 8:00 PM we'll catch his assistant, Amber Kendall, as she's leaving her aerobics class. Maybe talk to her near her car. He said she's not likely under surveillance there."

I looked first at my watch, then at Ginger, and then back to the chief.

"Chief, here's the plan. I'll try to contact Kendall at Green's Gym, and I'll let you know how the engagement turns out. Please get a search warrant from Judge Johansen if you can. I have a feeling the best way to turn Orb-Quartz's bomb off will be from inside Storm and Shield. If this Amber Kendall idea doesn't work out the way I'm guessing Orb-Quartz intends, we'll need default access to try from inside. *Tonight.*"

I quickly ran through my plan as the chief and Ginger nodded their understanding and agreement. Well, at least *most* of the time.

"Jack, what will you do if Orb-Quartz gets Kendall to walk you into a trap?"

Shit. I hadn't planned for Amber Kendall to be a bad actor.

"It doesn't kill your plan. I'm just saying you need to factor it in. We have to think about all options and risks here."

The chief looked at me with a deadly serious grimace on his face and said, "Jack, if we haven't gotten Orb-Quartz fixed by Friday at midnight, he's going to Carter's Mine. Got it?"

Ginger and I nodded in agreement as we looked at one another.

"Now, get going, Jack. I want to catch the judge before it gets too late. Ginger, you will come with me. When we go into Storm and Shield, I'll need you to help find what we need to fix Orb-Quartz's Nexus Core. Trying to get someone else up to speed in this story with technical skills will take too long."

We both nodded in acknowledgment again, and then I bolted down the hall to my office. I had a pocket radio with an old-fashioned earpiece that I used to listen to the Cincinnati Reds games late at night when on watch or other times when I found myself with more time than things to do with it.

When I got back in the room with Ginger and Orb-Quartz, I collected my things and said, "Ginger, I brought something for you." I started putting Orb-Quartz back into the bag.

I paused. Then I grinned broadly at Ginger as I opened my go bag, pulled out a Ruger Max pistol, and said, "Here, take this. It's loaded, but there's no round in the chamber."

She took the pistol, unloaded the magazine, and cleared the

weapon by pulling the slide to the rear, checking its action along the way.

"Got it, thank you," she said as she put the clip back into the pistol and then slipped the tiny pistol into her purse.

I smiled at her and said, "See you shortly." I exited the building and jumped into the truck.

I blasted across town, trying to reach the gym before Amber Kendall finished her workout so that I could catch her exiting the building.

As we were driving there, I asked Orb-Quartz to discuss aspects of his part of the plan with me. I wanted to elicit his thoughts, understand his thinking, and also measure out, in my mind, the likelihood of success.

"Good thinking, Quartz," I said as I contemplated what he had explained and also what Chief Borland had said to me about Amber Kendall setting me up. "Meeting your assistant away from her house is smart. What do you think Ms. Kendall can do for you?" I said.

"I hope she can tell me what's happened to Jessica Frontage, what's going on in general, and most importantly how to turn off this damned self-destruct function."

"Quartz, you've been missing for a long time, at least twelve weeks from my estimation. Is there any reason to believe she should not be trusted? I'm concerned about how to do this in a way that does not endanger the people of Wellspoint."

Quartz was quiet for a minute.

"Jack," Quartz began, "I'm planning to do this without putting you, Ginger, the people of Wellspoint, or Amber in danger. I'm certain I can trust Amber, but I do have to be careful in putting her in a bad position. I fear something is seriously wrong within the organization."

"Okay, Quartz, here's how this engagement's going to go down." I kept driving as we worked out the plan for engaging with Quartz's assistant. The more we talked, the more I realized there was a great deal to work out. If it was going to work out. If we were not going to be murdered *or exploded.*

I want to catch this murderer. And I'm getting closer. I can feel it.

Chapter 9

A very tall, slender brunette walked past me as I stood outside the gym's front door.

"Miss Kendall," I said as I stepped forward two short steps, closing the distance between us and tipping my fedora.

Damn, she's strikingly beautiful with unusually strong facial features. She was at least the same height as me, and I was 6' 4".

I smiled and held my wallet open so she could see my police badge and credentials.

She looked at the badge, then at me, and finally one more time back at the wallet.

"Officer...Stewart. Is there an issue?" she asked as other people went around us on their way to the parking lot.

"I'm not sure. It's probably nothing, but I would like to ask you a couple of questions. It should only take a few minutes."

She shifted her position a little to face me fully. "Okay, go ahead. Ask your questions," she replied evenly. She wasn't getting irritated, but she seemed to grow anxious as we became the only two people left standing in front of the gym.

"We need help with a person named Quartz Jacobs. I think he's your employer or your boss over at Storm and Shield. Is that right?"

"Ah. Okay, yes." She smiled tightly. "He is my boss. What sort of help do you need?" she said, putting her bag down and tilting her head to the side.

"Well, it's complicated," I said as I looked around for anything out of place or anyone who might have been within range of eavesdropping. "He's in a bit of danger, and he'd like to get your perspective on a problem he's dealing with," I said, looking directly into her eyes.

She focused her eyes on mine, and I could see she was starting to piece something together in her mind.

"Okay, Officer Stewart. I can give him a call on my cell phone and—"

"That won't be necessary," I said as I pointed to the earpiece in my ear.

She looked at me more carefully now, noting the earpiece.

"He said to ask you if there's a way to stop a running self-destruct process in his Nexus Core," I explained as I used my left hand to pull the Nexus Core partway out of my jacket pocket so that she could see it.

She looked down at the Nexus Core then back at me and seemed to be thinking really hard.

Her eyes were wide open, and she had a look on her face that grew more distrustful.

"Where did you get that?" she exclaimed.

"Miss Kendall, please focus for a moment. He also wants to know if his body is acting erratically. He's concerned that the significant time between syncs has caused his body to make mistakes, potentially doing something tragic to people in your office."

She looked around as she picked up her gym bag. Apparently, she'd made a decision.

"Officer Stewart, let's talk in my car, please."

I kept smiling and said, "Okay."

She turned and walked toward her car, and as we got a little closer, she used the remote to unlock her vehicle. I walked around to the passenger door, and we both got into the four-door SUV.

She started her car then reached under her seat and deftly pulled out a gun with her left hand. She pointed the gun at me and said, "Let me talk to him."

I raised both hands so she could see them and then carefully reached into my pocket with my right hand. I slowly pulled out the pocket AM FM radio and unplugged my earpiece. "Okay, Quartz, time for a three-way conversation," I said as I sat the little radio on the dash between Amber and me.

As her eyes moved to the radio on the dash, I quietly, crisply pulled the Glock out of my shoulder holster and pointed it at her.

She looked back at me, unblinking at the sight of the Glock, as Quartz started talking through the radio's small but capable speaker.

"Amber, I've got a self-destruct process running that I cannot stop. Can you help me with getting it under control?"

She looked thoughtful then looked over at me.

"Sir, this policeman knows far too much—"

Quartz cut her off. "It's okay, Amber. We've worked out an arrangement. Now, about the process, how can I turn it off?"

She looked at me and then reached to put her pistol back under the seat.

"If it's not resetting, are you receiving any feedback? Any messages?"

"No. I've tried a dozen times to reset the whole program, but it simply switches off and then back on. It displays a number briefly, and then the countdown timer reappears right where it was before I tried resetting it."

Amber tapped her finger against the console between us, but that looked to be only a fidgety move as she considered Orb-Quartz's comment. I put my pistol back into its holster.

"It sounds like you've been externally reconfigured using system override pins."

"What? By whom? That would indicate sabotage," Orb-Quartz retorted.

"Yes, sir, sabotage. I don't see how you could have configured yourself to execute those low-level commands. Most importantly, those commands are impossible for you to turn off. It requires a verification signal from the outside that corresponds to the processor-generated number that shows up during the reset. I can put your core into a dock back at the lab and probably provide the right sequence to reset it."

"Jack, can you please allow her to do this? I will hold up my end of our agreement. It's best for you that you do not go with us."

"Quartz, you know I can't let you out of my control. You are going into the mine if we can't turn this self-destruct off in a few hours. I have murders to solve and dead bodies stacking up. No, no. The plan is that you'll go into Storm and Shield, get the dock and whatever else you need, and we'll do the rest at the police station," I said, keeping an eye on both of Amber's hands.

"I can't do it that way. I need the computer at Storm and Shield," Amber replied.

"I didn't think about that," said Quartz.

I looked at her incredulously. "This fancy computer system

isn't portable?"

She gave me the side-eye and said, "Most *definitely* not portable. You'll have to come in then. I'll reset the self-destruct subsystem, and the situation will be resolved. And there will be no reason for his Nexus Core to depart the facility again," Amber said flatly as she looked at me.

"I still have several murders to solve. The Nexus is evidence and in police custody until I sort out what is going on," I said as I pulled out my cell phone and dialed the chief. He picked up right away, and I said, "Chief, I'm going into Storm and Shield. I'm with Amber and Orb-Quartz. I'll let you know when I go in, via text, and the same when I get out."

"Jack, wait for me. Don't go in alone. Remember what we talked about. I don't have the search warrant yet."

"Search warrant?" said Orb-Quartz.

"Yes," I replied, stressed that Quartz had been able to hear the chief. "The backup plan is to go into the facility and investigate what the hell's going on in there and look for any clues that tie the recent spate of murders to Storm and Shield or potentially Quartz."

"I'm driving to the judge's house now. I have to go. Call me before you go in, Jack. You need backup," said the chief as he hung up.

"Amber, what happened to Jessica?" said Orb-Quartz through the radio.

Amber was quiet as she looked from the radio to me and then back to the radio as if Orb-Quartz could see her. "I don't completely understand what happened. I was told there was an accident and her car drove off the road and into Wellspoint Lake. I was told your Nexus Core was taken to an offsite location for protection."

"Accident? What kind of accident? Who told you my Nexus was taken off-site?" asked Orb-Quartz.

"I don't know the accident's details, but Quartz was involved, at least the police think so since they took him in for questioning twice," she replied carefully.

"Is he behaving erratically? Did he kill Jessica? What's going on back at Storm and Shield?"

"There's been a lot of work on Project Renaissance. There have been some successes but some issues as well. I don't really know, as I'm not authorized to work with that team on that set of problems. I think it was something related to that effort. Mr. Drake and Mr. Paulus have been in the facility a lot lately and—"

I broke into the conversation. "Let's discuss on the way to your facility."

"No," said Quartz. "We've got to wait until after 9:00 PM. That will give us the best chance to get you in and out safely."

Amber continued, "Since Flint returned from off-site, things have been very different. He's been blindly supporting that new specialist you hired, Dr. Rockwell. And your behavior has been somewhat—"

"What?" asked Orb-Quartz.

"Aggressive," Amber said. "And perhaps a little callous."

We all sat quietly for an uncomfortable minute.

"New plan," said Orb-Quartz. "Amber, drive home and change clothes."

"Why?" she asked.

"You are going on a date tonight with Jack. Then you remember that you need to reset the serializer on one of the Project Jupiter systems so that it can run overnight and be ready when you get into work Friday morning."

"Okay, but won't the security system recognize Jack when he

enters the building?" she said as she looked at me.

"No, Jack will be wearing a hat and a patch over one eye because he was injured this morning. Jack, we'll have to stop at a drugstore along the way and purchase an eyepatch. The system will not detect him, but you must get him from the front door to the lab stairwell quickly. I don't want Arthur to contact Quartz secretly."

"Okay," she said.

I considered what Quartz proposed and thought it might be a decent way to get to the bottom of all of this, including the murder, and I felt a bit more like I could trust Amber and the voice on the radio. I looked at Amber and said, "We stick together all the time. You don't use any phones or computers until we get out of the facility after you turn off the self-destruct system."

Before she could say anything, Orb-Quartz said, "Agreed. This will work, Amber. You have to trust me."

She smiled flatly and said, "I trust you, sir. I'm just concerned about how we handle anything unforeseen with the guards there and long-term with the police."

"I have a plan for the police that will work for everyone. You'll have to do your best to get Jack and me into the building. Deal with the guards. Once I'm in the dock, I can connect to the computer and sort out a few details, and you can help me turn off this self-destruct program. Let's get going, Amber."

"Yes, sir," Amber said, and she started the SUV's engine and drove us out of the gym parking lot.

I certainly hope this plan works. We've got to find out who's murdering these people, I thought.

Chapter 10

We arrived at Amber's apartment and talked a little while discussing how to get past the Storm and Shield guards.

Amber's plan was good. She would use her valid credentials and personal relationship with one of the guards to help me bypass security, creating a distraction if necessary.

I looked around and realized her apartment was nicely furnished and spacious.

"Nice place. Storm and Shield must be doing something right," I said at a low volume.

"It beats a dreary home in the suburbs. I've done that. It's no fun," she replied.

She walked into the bedroom. I followed from a safe distance. It felt awkward going into her bedroom.

"I'm going to take a quick shower. I can't go on a date all sweaty," she said, smiling at me as she put air quotes around the word "date."

"Okay. No phone calls, please," I said as I stood near her bedroom door.

She turned to face me. "I'll adhere to our agreement."

Turning her back to me once more, she stripped off her workout clothes, tossing them toward a hamper across the room. I tried not to notice how naked she was, but it wasn't easy. She had a nice body. Very fit. *Okay, Jack, stop looking at her perfect body,* I thought.

Then, without ceremony, she turned and stepped into the bathroom out of my visual range. I heard the flow of water from the shower.

I small-talked with Orb-Quartz as we turned our discussion to the present situation.

"She'll do her part, Jack," said Orb-Quartz.

I considered Orb-Quartz's statement for a moment.

"I think the real question is if you trust her," I replied. A moment of silence elapsed, so I continued, "If she's in on the murders and had a part in killing Jessica Frontage, she could be setting both of us up."

More silence.

"I've considered this, Jack. When I learned that I was found in the possession of a very dead Jessica Frontage, I became immediately concerned that I could not fully trust anyone except, apparently, a lanky, thirty-something policeman named Jack, who I've never met."

"Right. So our agreement is still in place? I can trust you?"

"Yes. You hold up your end of our bargain, and I'll fulfill my part. I still don't think my body has committed these murders but—"

"Okay, Jack, time for dinner," said Amber as she exited the bathroom wearing only a towel. She walked to the dresser and started taking clothes out and putting them on under her towel.

The towel hit the floor, and I turned to face away from her.

Trying to refocus my brain away from her beautiful physique, I asked Orb-Quartz some questions about his power supply and how far below ground he'd need to be in order to safely detonate, but he was unsure. He expressed a great desire to solve the whole self-destruct mechanism prior to having to figure that out. "Jack, even though I'm a computerized device, I still think the same way a person does. I don't want to die."

Smiling, I said, "I understand that. Just making backup plans as needed. Dropping you into that mine isn't my idea of solving the problem."

"No dropping, Jack," Quartz responded with a humorous lilt to his voice.

"Right. *No more* dropping," I said.

A fully dressed Amber looked at me and asked, "No *more* dropping?"

"It's a long story, but I dropped his Nexus Core a couple of times down at the police station while interrogating the other Quartz."

Amber froze for a moment, considering what I'd said. Amber started walking my way and said, "No wonder you are experiencing challenges with your systems, sir. Nexus Cores are extremely delicate."

I nodded, but not with as much comprehension as I'd like to have, because I couldn't help but notice how pretty she looked in the clothes she was wearing. She had on a tight skirt, well above the knees, and a low-cut, sleeveless top that showed her thin but muscular arms, neck, and shoulders. The skirt left little to imagine about what her lower body looked like above the dark, high-heeled shoes adorning each foot. Her dark, silky hair was pinned up on her head, which, coupled with the perfume she was wearing... Well, she was a mesmerizing display of beauty.

She noticed my stare and said, "This is me trying to be distracting."

I turned my head a degree or two, raised an eyebrow, and three words stumbled out of my mouth. "It's. Very. Distracting."

"Good," she replied with a brilliantly beautiful smile.

"All right, come on. Let's get going, you two," interrupted Orb-Quartz.

And we departed.

We drove across town in Amber's car, stopping at a drugstore along the way so that I could pick up an eye patch. Apparently, their security system would not be able to identify me if it could not see both eyes when scanning my facial features.

"It's after 9 PM. Amber, park in front of the main doors in the curbside loading zone," said Orb-Quartz as we approached the building. "Remember, Jack, you are a visiting scientist and Amber's boyfriend. It's best if you don't speak too much. You know, don't be memorable. When we get into the lab, I'll modify logs in the security systems so Quartz isn't tipped off."

"Got it," I said. "Shut up and smile. I can do that."

We parked in front of the building and exited the car calmly. Amber walked slowly because of the high-heeled shoes she was wearing, so I took the opportunity to look around the area. *Very few folks are on the street, and really, there's not much going on for a Thursday night after 9 PM*, I thought.

Amber used her access badge on the big double-door card reader. It buzzed to life as she pulled the right side door open, allowing me to enter first.

The stairwell was dark, and I glanced back at Amber with a questioning look. "The lights will come on when we walk down the stairs," Amber explained.

We started to descend the stairs, and when we reached the foyer at the bottom, a guard stood up from his desk and said, "Good evening, Ms. Hunt." His eyes immediately scanned me from head to toe as he said, "Sir, I can't say as I recognize you. Do you have some ID with you that I can check?"

Before I could reply, Amber jumped in. "He's with me, Arthur. He's the genetic specialist I was telling you about. He walked into a cabinet at the dinner tonight, and we had to get him a few stitches."

I smiled gently as I looked from Amber back to the guard.

"Arthur James, this is Doctor Quincy Baker. Quincy, say hello to Arthur James. He runs evening security at our main facility. I just need to check the serializer on one of the Project Jupiter systems. I want to make sure it's running so I can see the results tomorrow morning. It takes about nine hours to run," she told James.

I nodded to Amber, acknowledging her stated purpose for the visit, and turned to face the guard. Arthur and I shook hands as Amber typed an entry into the computer, probably registering me as a guest.

"Dr. Baker, it's a pleasure to meet you, and it's good to finally meet you in person. Amber talks about you often."

I smiled back at the guard. "It's great to meet you as well," I said as I tried to keep the small talk generic.

Amber started walking across the foyer to the second set of stairs that led to the lab saying, "C'mon, Quincy. Let's get in, get this done, and get out."

I smiled at Arthur, issued a thank you nod, then turned and followed Amber to the lab.

Amber badged in through the main double doors and then into the lab itself. When we entered the lab, I slowly scanned the place. There was technical-looking stuff sitting everywhere. All kinds of electronics, tools, beakers, microscopes, and flasks. All kinds of science-looking shit. *This kind of stuff gives me a headache.*

Amber pointed across the room, where I saw a familiar piece

of equipment. It was one of the Nexus Core docking stations, and it was connected via cables to a wall plug. "Jack, put the Nexus Core there on that dock. This shouldn't take long. Sir, I need you to generate one of those reset numbers."

I moved across the room and placed Orb-Quartz onto the dock. I pulled out my pocket radio and whispered, "Quartz, you are connected now. Can you provide Amber with one of those reset numbers?"

Orb-Quartz's digitized voice came through my portable radio with some words elongated, as if his system was concurrently processing tons of new input. "Jaaack. Yees, I'm connnnnected. Pleaase. Give. Me. A. Momeeent."

Amber returned from wherever she had gone with what looked like a calculator with a set of small jumper wires with thin, needle-like ends attached. "Okay, he seems to be connected to the computer and functioning properly."

"Yes, Amber, I'm okay. The number I see after attempting a self-destruct reset is 0732113."

Amber punched the number into the small, calculator-looking device. She then plugged in a long wire that ran from an outlet in the nearby wall into the device. She leaned over Quartz's Nexus Core, looking for places to plug in the small, needle-like tips. "Dad, I cannot see the service ports. Can you please raise the light level a degree or two?" No sooner had she finished her sentence than the cracks and fine lines on the surface of Quartz's Nexus Core started emitting a dim green hue. "Okay, here we go," she said as she plugged the tips into two tiny holes in the Nexus Core. Amber watched the readings on the small calculator device, punched in a sequence of numbers, and hit what looked like an enter key. "Okay, that's it, sir. That should reset your self-destruct mechanism after you run a full reboot of that subsystem."

I looked at Amber with astonishment then down at the small device that resembled a calculator. "Well, that doesn't look so big and unportable," I said, pointing at the small box. This was a reference to an earlier conversation where she said we had to bring Orb-Quartz back here because the computer needed to reset the self-destruct mechanism was not portable.

Amber tilted her head to the side with a smile. She then placed the box on the table and said, "Follow me, Jack."

I followed Amber toward the back of the lab through a small doorway that led to a large rectangular room. On one side of the room, there were a few tables and chairs. Along the entire length of the other side was a long, rectangular-looking system of some kind. It had all manner of old-fashioned-looking screens, light bulbs, dials, levers, and even a couple of small keyboard-looking devices mounted on the side. It was at least ten meters long and at least two meters high.

She pointed at the old-looking yet massive device.

"*That's* the computer?" I asked incredulously. "It looks like someone strapped a bunch of 1960s televisions to an old ENIAC."

Amber folded her arms, smiled, and nodded affirmatively.

"Amber!" Quartz called out, so we briskly walked back into the main lab room.

"I'm here," she responded.

"Amber, I need you to go out and reboot the visitor registra-tion computer. To do that, you hold down the control-alt-delete keys. A dialogue will pop up. Just click the reboot option. I've cleaned all the security logs, but there will be cached records there I cannot get rid of. I don't want to leave detailed evidence of our visit. Please do it quickly."

She looked from Orb-Quartz to me with a puzzled look on her face. Then she appeared to have an epiphany. "Okay, I'll bring Arthur a cup of coffee. It's something I occasionally do when working late. I'll spill as I hand it to him, and when he backs away to wipe it up, I'll quickly reboot the computer."

"Good idea. Before you go, please get my backup access card from the third drawer of my desk and give it to Jack. Jack, I need you to take me downstairs into one of our research vaults. I'll walk you through how to get there. Amber, please wait here for us when you are done."

Amber disappeared from view and then returned with an access card that had Quartz's name on it. She handed it to me and smiled broadly, saying, "I'll be back."

"Jack, pick me up. I need you to carry me with you. Time is short."

I lifted Orb-Quartz up off the dock. Man, was he hot.

"You're really warm. Is everything alright? What about the self-destruct? Did that get fixed after you rebooted?"

"Yes, Jack. I'm back to my old, healthy self. I downloaded a lot of data, which always creates heat. Please proceed back through the computer room door. When you get there, turn right. You should see a large vault door. I want you to use this keycard after you punch in the security code 1771471 on the door's keypad to open the door. We only have thirteen minutes to get in and out, because that's as much time as I have to safely erase the security systems event logs."

"Okay, got it," I said, looking back toward the door we'd need to go through. I walked through the computer room and turned right. *Yep, there was a big-assed door with a lot of security-looking gadgets on it.* "Where'd you dig up that computer?" I mused as I punched in the security code after receiving a green light. I held the key card up to the security badge reader. The vault door unlocked.

"You'll have to pull it open, Jack. And don't close it completely. We don't want it to lock, as this key card won't get us back out if the door closes behind you. It's my backup access card."

I pulled the door open, walked through, and looked around on the other side. I whistled at the sight of it. The huge room was dimly lit, and there was even more lab gear.

"I told you, Jack. The computer and this technology are very, very old. I'm very old."

"Great, well, did you find any leads on the murder? Any log entries or other insights?" I asked as I plucked a nearby lab stool and posted it in the doorway to prevent the door from closing.

"Yes, I found some fascinating information, but I'm still working through the data that I downloaded from the computer. I should have some insights shortly."

"Great. What are we looking for down here?"

"I'm looking for evidence that corroborates a brewing theory I've got about what's going on with my company," Quartz said. "So go all the way to the end and turn left. We need to enter one last lab room. It's called the Olympus Lab. If the door isn't open, use the code and key card combination again. Please remember to prop the door open."

"Okay. So what exactly are we looking for?" I asked as I quietly crept down the dimly lit room, stopping at the end and turning left.

"Let's see what you see when we get into the room, Jack. I don't honestly know what we'll find, but I think it's best for you to do the investigating. Whatever doesn't fit in there is likely the key to solving both our issues."

I started to get concerned that Orb-Quartz was slowly walking me into a trap. The kind of trap that was going to get me, or any other sucker, caught deep in the bowels of a super-secure building. I walked to the large door, used the code and key card again, and entered the Olympus lab. "Holy shit," I said.

"What? What is it, Jack?" asked Quartz.

"This room is full of huge, fluid-filled test tubes with…with some animals in them."

"Jack, please walk around the room and tell me what kind of animals you see."

"Quartz, these look like people. Young versions of people like you! People with four fingers," I said as my heart started pounding and a cold sweat broke out over my body. It was very eerie to see these things.

"Please don't panic, Jack. These must be the clones Dr. Alexander and the Renaissance team have been working on. This is how my people have existed for so long. We grew numerous clones of ourselves in a reactor like this, and then we use the NeuraSync computer upstairs to install the matrix from our Nexus Core into the brain of the clone."

"Who knows about this? About you? Does the government know?"

"That's complicated, but we have an agreement with a few governments. Please, Jack, keep looking around. Walk to the back end of the room and verify you've checked everywhere."

"Okay, okay, this is definitely freaking me out."

"I understand, Jack. Please focus. Do you see anything unusual?"

This last comment caused me to stop in my tracks, and I slowly looked down at Orb-Quartz in bewilderment.

"You've got to be shitting me. Everything down here is unusual!" I whispered hoarsely.

"Yes. Sorry about that. I'd imagine so. Please keep looking around, Jack. Time is short."

I started walking around again, taking pictures with my cell phone camera. A couple of silent minutes later, I ran into a seriously concerning sight. "Shit. Shit. What the hell?" I blurted out.

"What is it, Jack? What do you see?"

"It's the chief. I mean, I think it's Chief Borland. He's in one of these big, person-sized test tubes." I rushed to the massive glass tube containing Chief Borland's body. It looked like the chief for sure. "Did your body do this, Quartz?" I asked. My heart pounded so hard I could feel it in my head.

"Jack, please calm yourself. You've got to look at the body carefully. This is most likely a clone of Chief Borland."

I considered what Orb-Quartz said and calmed myself a notch. *Yep,* I thought, *this looks like a clone of the chief. It's a much younger version of him now that I look at it a little more closely.* I stared into the tube looking at the cloned body of Chief Borland. It had a hose connected through a small mouthpiece, presumably for breathing inside the thick, beige, fluid-filled tube. There were several dozen wires attached to some sensors all over his body. I felt sick as I wondered if these people were trying to replace the chief. What if they did already? If they could use this clone and put one of their minds into his body—

A lot of ugly possibilities flashed through my mind. Had they done this before? Who have they replaced? At what levels in our population have they replaced people with their clones? The president? Congressmen? "Quartz, have you replaced humans with your own clones in our society? What are you? Aliens?" I asked dejectedly, not expecting to get an honest answer. I was feeling very unsettled. Very much like everything I thought I could count on in the world was shaken.

"No, Jack. Our matrices, that is, our neural networks, won't work in your brain. We have two additional organs in our brains that the NeuraSync system relies upon for transfer and resilience."

"Then why in the hell are you cloning the chief?" I asked incredulously.

"I do not know why this occurred, Jack. I did not authorize this activity. It is strictly against our laws. This does, however, confirm what I was most concerned about."

"Oh yeah, and what is that?" I asked through a frustrated exhalation.

"Someone is using my lab to do bad things, and they want me out of the way. Also, I strongly suspect that Jessica Frontage lost her life trying to protect me."

"Protect you from whom?" I asked.

"I'm not sure. But whoever it is must be responsible for the deaths in the case that you are working on, as well as responsible for cloning Chief Borland. Whoever is responsible is not following our laws or is knowingly violating them. My brother and I wouldn't do that."

I took a couple more cellphone pictures of things in the room.

"Time's up, Jack. We've got to get back to the main lab. We need to get out of the facility. I can only cover a certain number of security logs from the main security system. Please be certain to lock the Olympus lab and the main lab doors. You need to shut each door then use the code and key card to lock the doors behind you."

"Gladly," I said as I mentally parsed through a number of what-if scenarios.

Chapter 11

I put Orb-Quartz back onto the dock and started nosing around the main lab room waiting for Amber to return.

"Okay, that's it. The Olympus and main lab access logs have all been erased. The remaining security logs will auto-delete in about eight minutes. That's how long we've got to get Amber and get out of here."

I considered Orb-Quartz's words and thought ruefully about whether this whole thing was a trap or if I was being deceived. I decided to go along for now. "Okay. Amber's not back yet. Do I wait on her?"

"No, Jack, we've got to get out of here. I'm not confident that Quartz hasn't been tipped to our presence. Put in your earpiece so that I can talk to you. I may be able to help you get by Arthur without incident. Please grab her purse and anything we've left behind."

I scanned the area and grabbed Amber's purse. "Okay." I plugged in the headphones and pushed the earpiece into my ear. I organized Orb-Quartz and Amber's purse and headed out the doors, up the stairs, and back into the main hallway. As I approached, I saw Amber talking with Arthur. I walked up to them and smiled gingerly at each of them, trying to play it cool while my mind was screaming, *Get out now*! Then I turned to

Amber and said, "I'd like to come back another time and see where you do your experimentation, if that works for you."

Amber looked at me, puzzled for a microsecond, and then said, "Yes, I'm sorry I couldn't take you into the lab's experimentation area. That's where we store Storm and Shield's proprietary data." She noticed the purse in my hand and deftly adapted to the situation by asking, "Is your eye feeling better?"

I smiled again at her as I gently touched the eyepatch with my left hand. "Yes, thank you for the ointment. I appreciate you letting me use your restroom to check my eye. I'm such a damned klutz."

She turned back to Arthur and said, "Okay, Arthur, I'll see you in about eight hours."

He smiled at her and raised his cup of coffee a few inches, saying, "Yes, ma'am, and thank you for the coffee. We'll see you in the morning."

I extended my right hand, and Arthur accepted the handshake.

"It was great to meet you finally, Doctor Baker."

I nodded and said, "You as well, Arthur. Have a great evening." I slowly turned to Amber, handing her the purse.

We walked up the main stairway and out the double doors.

"We need to get out of here. Your father is worried that Quartz may have been watching the facility closely."

"Okay, Jack. Did you two find anything?"

I glanced over at her and smiled grimly. "Yes, we found quite a bit." We got into the car and drove off.

"Where to?" asked Amber.

"To the police station," I said. "I texted the chief and let him know we were on the way." Orb-Quartz's voice came in over the car's speakers, so I pulled the earpiece out of my ear. He started catching Amber and me up on what he'd found. Electricity consumption was way up, among other inconsistencies with the Project Renaissance lab data. We finally ended up on a topic I was internally concerned about.

"Jack, how well do you know Chief Borland?"

I winced internally, considering what Orb-Quartz had posited. Seconds elapsed. "The chief hired me onto the force about seven years ago. I came straight out of the Army after doing two tours in the war," I quipped abruptly.

"I can understand this is a difficult topic, but we have to consider the chance that he's been compromised or perhaps replaced. Apparently, he somehow discovered the dead bodies, including Jessica. He then recovered my Nexus Core. Recent security logs show his fingerprints were found in the main lab, which is unusual and indicative that someone enabled that. Something isn't right about his knowledge and access."

"I trust him," I said with finality in my voice as I tried to convince myself.

We all sat quietly for a minute or so.

Finally, I verbalized my most concerning thoughts, "There was a recent incident where the chief came busting out of Storm and Shield. He later claimed he had some gaps in his memory, and it was troubling him. Anything in your security logs about that?"

"No, Jack, I don't see any records indicating a visit occurred. That's the problem. Do you know specifically what day it was? Or a time frame?"

I considered whether Orb-Quartz was telling me the truth. I realized I had no way to verify anything the chief or Orb-Quartz were telling me. And there was the whole missing W-shaped birthmark issue.

"Wednesday morning around 7:00 AM," I replied.

"Okay, I see some... No, that's not it. No. I do not see anything at that time. Let me check elsewhere."

Seconds passed.

Orb-Quartz continued, "Okay, someone clearly erased the security log events in hour chunks. Yes, there's a pattern of logs missing from different log types. All within the same time range. Something occurred early Wednesday morning around 3:30 to 04:15 AM. Later, there's a large chunk of logs missing from 7:07 to 9:17 AM."

"Well, that's something. That could confirm the activity. Who has the computer privileges to erase the logs? Have you found anything that can help us understand if and how the chief could be mixed up in this?"

"No, Jack. Unfortunately, there are no records of the cloning activity, and there is no assigned staff to manage that body. Very unusual. Unfortunately, I'm the only person with the ability to delete log events."

Amber piped in, "I've not been into the Olympus lab since your nexus was removed. I did try about four weeks ago, but I noticed my access was turned off. When I asked why, your brother said there was an accident and that everyone's access was disabled until he got the situation cleaned up and under control. I didn't really give it a second thought. I was just returning a microscope filter to one of the cabinets."

After nearly a minute of contemplation, Orb-Quartz started a new conversation. "Jack, I need you to help me get my body back."

I looked at Amber as she glanced at me.

"How does that help me solve my case? Regardless, how the heck am I supposed to do that? Isn't all the gear you need back at your headquarters building? There's no way we are getting back in there without being noticed by Quartz or Flint."

"There is another option. It's very close hold, but we have an off-site facility outside of town. That facility is capable of executing the transfer. And with the updated memories, I could tell you if I was the murderer. Quartz should listen to you as a policeman and submit to the transfer session."

"Do you trust having your Nexus Core updated? I mean, what if some other actor has overwritten your body from their Nexus Core with malicious data? Maybe that's what Jessica was trying to protect you from. Wouldn't that malicious network data overwrite your Nexus Core's neural network?" I asked.

Orb-quartz was quiet for several seconds.

"If I don't receive the body's input, I'll lose months of life experiences. Regardless, I still need to sync my matrix into my body. Given what has occurred thus far and the possibility of sabotage, I think it's wise to implement all the precautions possible to ensure my cognitive integrity. Amber, you'll have to ground my body's output so my Nexus Core doesn't receive any updates from my brain during the neural inductive sync session. Just a one-way sync to the body. It's a delicate configuration that must be performed manually."

Amber's face contorted into a worried look as she continued driving us to the police station.

"What is it, Amber? Are you on board with this?" I asked.

Amber was silent for a few seconds and finally responded, "I don't like modifying the Nexus Core during the neural inductive update process. It's very dangerous. The NeuraSync system is designed to operate in a balance. If that balance gets corrupted or offset for too long, it can damage the Nexus Core's neural network. There's a tremendous amount of power involved and tons of data transferred. I don't like it."

Orb-Quartz was quick to reply, "The other option is I take the full transfer and hope there are no malicious inputs or sequences found. Here, I'd be counting on the strength of my own system to repair and overwrite malicious injects or any anomalous connectivity."

We were all quiet for at least a full minute of time.

"Okay," I said, "I'm in. We'll have to sort that piece out. Quartz, what happens if he doesn't submit willingly? How'd you intend for me to subdue you long enough to do this transfer? I'm a pretty big guy, but if you have the kind of combat experience you claim, how am I supposed to bring you down?"

Quartz replied, "We need a powerful stun gun, Jack. That would make the difference between success and failure. My people are very, very vulnerable to strong electrical shock. Much more susceptible than humans. I presume you have one of these as part of your official police equipment?"

"I do. I have one in my truck, which is back at Green's Gym."

"Then may I recommend we skip going to the police station? Let's go to the off-site and prepare the system for full operation. We'll need to strategize how to lure Quartz to the site alone, without his private security detail."

I considered Quartz's words and looked over at Amber. We stopped at a red light, and she looked back at me. I could see she was scared.

"What do you think, Amber?"

She turned to look back at the road and said, "As uncomfortable as it may be to consider, it might be good to avoid Chief Borland, at least until we have some more facts about the situation."

I pondered her thoughts. I considered what I was getting myself into. I was trying to avoid stepping into a trap. This situation was bizarre. I didn't know who I could trust. I didn't know any of these people. On the other hand, I had known the chief for years. One thing was undoubtedly evident. I was growing tired of being Orb-Quartz's keeper. It was time to get Orb-Quartz back into his body. From there, I thought we could sort out many of the issues and finally figure out who murdered Jessica Frontage and the other three folks with her. There was also the matter of the two dead bodies found at the golf course.

"Okay. Let's grab the Taser out of my truck and head out to your off-site. I'll contact the chief and tell him we've changed plans. We'll meet him in the morning."

We'd stopped so I could pick up my service-issued stun gun, a TASER X26P which was in my go-bag. Then we gassed up Amber's car at a local fuel station, grabbing some coffee and some very unhealthy gas station snacks. Apparently, there was no food where we were heading.

I decided to call the chief, and he was very irritated that the judge wouldn't approve the search warrant for him to search Storm and Shield. The judge had said to come back tomorrow before lunch with a better case. Nothing was happening tonight, so he sent Ginger home. I talked to the chief for about ten minutes. He seemed unusually stressed, but nothing came up that seemed unusual or indicated that he was in any way compromised. Given our years of working together, I knew something was off, but it was hard to think it might be with the chief. Yet here I was, trusting Amber and Orb-Quartz.

During the call to the chief, Ginger texted me to say that she was not feeling well and needed to get out of town for a while. She said she'd grabbed a few things from home and headed to her mom's house for the weekend. She said she'd call me on Monday when she returned. *This whole situation must have been pretty intense for a girl like Ginger*, I thought.

"How long until we reach your off-site facility?" I asked no one in particular.

"About an hour," Amber replied. "Wow, Chief Borland was really wound up!"

"Agreed. Jack, did anything unusual come up during the conversation?" asked Orb-Quartz.

"No, not really. He was animated about the judge refusing to give him a search warrant, which was a little unusual but not unprecedented," I replied as I plugged the TASER X26P into the car's USB socket to top off its charge. "So *how* do we intend to lure Quartz to the site?" I asked.

"The plan is for Amber to call in tomorrow morning around 7:00 and let Quartz know that she's working from the off-site location all day and asked him to come out and help her review some strange security logs from the security system. He'll come. I'm certain of it."

"Okay. How do we ensure *only he* shows up? What about his security detail?" I asked.

"He'll be suspicious of what she's doing out here, but I'm pretty sure he'll leave his security detail behind if it's only Amber at the facility."

"And why is that?" I asked.

"Because Quartz trusts Amber. And everything back at the facility will check out if someone gets concerned about Dr. Baker's unusual visit. I created all the appropriate entries for Dr. Baker to cover Amber's visit. Including logging the opening and closing of the executive bathroom that corresponds to when you would have used the room to treat your ailing eye."

"Okay.... What's so special about Amber?" I asked as I looked over at her behind the wheel.

Several seconds elapsed.

"Jack, she's my daughter."

"What?" I asked in amazement.

"Don't you think that's something you might have shared a bit earlier in the story, Quartz?" I asked, sounding irritated, as I felt someone leading me around and using me to solve their personal problems while murder victims stacked up across our town.

"Jack, a coherent Quartz would not harm Amber. But few know that she's my daughter. I think you could understand why I don't want many people to know."

"I don't understand any of this. Who is Amber's mother? Where is she?"

"Jack, Amber's mother was—"

"Well?"

"A human named Isabella Garcia. She died eight years ago."

"So your...species and humans can procreate?"

"Yes, Jack. It's not easy, but in vitro fertilization has worked."

"What are you guys, Quartz? Are you aliens?"

"Not aliens, Jack. Technically, we were here before humans. Thousands of years before humans."

"Well, if that's the case, then how come we don't see a bunch of four-fingered giant skeletons all over the world being dug up and highlighted as the first inhabitants of this planet?"

"Jack, our people lived and settled in what you would call Antarctica thousands of years ago. If you dig up the ground where our cities and towns were, you'll find a very large number of skeletons there. Our society has declined in population over its many years of existence. That's why our leaders developed the cloning strategy to save us from extinction."

I shook my head, trying to wrap my mind around all this new information.

"I realize this is a lot to process, Jack. Why don't you get some rest on the way to the off-site facility?" suggested Amber in a careful, polite tone.

"In the last three days, I've learned that humans are not alone on this planet, let alone in this solar system. I've learned we have orb people from, apparently, the continent of Antarctica, who live thousands of years by inhabiting cloned bodies. Call me crazy, but I'm not feeling very sleepy."

My frustration settled down a bit, so I continued with a more resolute tone, "I've also learned that someone wanted those four people dead bad enough to murder them, pack them in the victim's car, and sink them to the bottom of Wellspoint Lake. I don't know about the other two bodies. One of them had one of those proprietary chips clutched in her hand. What do those chips do anyway?"

"The chips that sit on the Nexus Core dock?" asked Amber.

"Yes, the ones that sit in specific positions around the top of the dock."

"Those are bridge chips used for extending a Nexus Core's memory. Typically, they contain specialized knowledge, experiences, or skills."

"That's right, Jack. I have several dozen of them. For example, if I want to remember specific details about quantum mechanics experiments my people performed a thousand years ago, I have a chip that contains the appropriately formatted neural network layers that are designed to be accessible from our Nexus Cores. I even have one that contains memories of Amber's mother, although it's too painful to expose myself to those memories right now."

I considered what they'd told me long and hard. An advanced species living thousands of years before modern humans was a difficult pill to swallow. "So can you store your body's memories for the last twelve weeks into one of those chips and safely access it later? Perhaps that's better than losing the data."

"Yes, I see where you are going. Perhaps it could be done, but it wouldn't be done in a way that I could reintegrate it into my mind. You see, these bridge chips store fact-of-type data. It's like looking at an encyclopedia. Facts, figures, video, that sort of thing would be retrievable, but the experience of the events would not be available."

"So you could read about what occurred but not fully experience it? Is that it?"

"Yes, Jack, that's mostly right," responded Orb-Quartz.

Amber slowed the car, looking for something specific along the side of the road. Apparently she found her marker, and we sharply turned left off the highway onto a gravel road that snaked around a bend or two. About half a mile down the road, we stopped in front of a small building nestled in the forest. Its frontage had two windows and a small set of stairs leading to the front door.

We got out of the car, and I looked around. I didn't recognize exactly where we were. I could hear the Miami River nearby. It was pitch dark out here. The building had a tiny security light shining what little light it could afford in our direction. *Not much here*, I thought. "Out of town and by the river. What's up with this location?"

Amber smiled and grabbed a few things out of the back seat of the car.

Orb-Quartz's voice came through my pocket radio speaker, saying, "Power, Jack. We've used this facility for years, before electricity was a thing for the people of Wellspoint, Ohio. We use the river to generate the enormous amounts of electricity we need."

"I was wondering about that. And about how your technology works and where you got the power to run all the gadgets that I saw in your lab."

"Let's get inside. I'm exhausted," Amber said.

"Agreed, I'm tired as well," I replied as I grabbed my things from the back seat and we headed into the building.

Amber used a key to unlock the front door, and we went inside. When we entered the room, a faintly audible beeping sound started emanating from a speaker on the wall. She immediately walked over and reset a rather sophisticated-looking alarm system, while I looked around the room a little. It didn't have too much in terms of furnishings. Two large desks and some old computer peripherals were lying about in the room. Amber walked toward the center of the room and opened a secondary door, which led to a somewhat steep-looking stairwell. She looked back at me and said, "Let's go downstairs. The alarm will turn itself back on shortly."

We descended the dimly lit stairs and entered a foyer containing three doors. Amber walked up to the doorway on the right and punched in a security code. She then waved her security badge in front of the card reader. Metal tumblers clicked and whirred as the door unlocked. We stepped through the doorway, and Amber locked it behind us. I noted she also pushed a mechanical bolt across the door and then switched on several lights near the entryway. "Wow, nothing's getting in here now," I said.

Amber smiled and said, "Yes, we are fairly safe here. Jack, let's power up the computer and get Dad onto the system's dock."

"That would be perfect, Amber," Orb-Quartz said through the portable radio in my pocket.

We turned and walked into the large bay. Amber narrated as

we walked toward the end of the room.

"The lab is at the end of this bay. These side rooms were for the staff to live in when this facility was active. There are beds and basic furnishings. Go ahead and take a look," she said as she continued toward the back of the room.

I stopped and pushed one of the doors open, switched on the lights, and walked in.

It looked like a small hotel room with a full-sized bed, dresser, full bathroom, closet, and small countertop with a sink and what looked like a single stovetop burner. *Not bad*, I thought.

I caught up with Amber as she turned on the power in the lab and sat Orb-Quartz into the dock lit up with power.

"Okay, I'm going to go change clothes. I'll leave you two to strategize for tomorrow," Amber said as she smiled and turned to exit the room.

I turned to look at Quartz. Then I looked over the wall and saw a camera. "Can you see through that camera, Quartz?"

Quartz's voice replied from a speaker on the wall. "I can. Believe me, being able to see in the local environment is a very handy attribute."

I smiled at the camera and shook my head ruefully. "Is she your only child?"

"Yes, Jack. She's very special to me. Given the centuries of cloning, it's difficult for us to have offspring within our own species, but when I met Amanda's mom, I broke my own personal rule about getting into a relationship with a human."

"Yes, I can see several issues. In particular, your life is reasonably perpetual, and she's going to die."

"Precisely. Well, Jack, can you please insert the bridge chip you found in that dead body's hand? I'd like to review the information tonight while you and Amber get some rest."

"Sure." I walked over and positioned the bridge chip onto the dock the way Chief Borland had shown me.

Orb-Quartz and I chatted for a while as I triple-checked the TASER X26P's charge level and other components. "What's on the chip?" I asked.

"It's some kind of research. I can't access all of it though; some parts appear to be encrypted. That's odd," Quartz replied. "Jack, you should rest. It's been a long day. Tomorrow will be very busy."

"Agreed," I said, smiling. "I need some sleep."

I left the lab and walked back to one of the rooms, turned on the light, and dropped my go-bag onto the dresser. I took my shirt off, threw it onto the dresser, rooted around, found a towel, and then decided I could use a shower. Fifteen minutes later, I was settling into bed when Amber stepped into my doorway wearing what appeared to be nothing more than a shirt.

I looked up at her. "You okay?" I asked.

"Yeah, I'm okay. I just wanted to stop by and say thank you for helping me to rescue my father. When he disappeared from the lab, I thought I'd lost him forever." She stepped into the room, leaning over, put her hands on the bed next to me, and sat down on the edge of the bed.

I looked up at her, smiling. "Happy to help."

She leaned over and kissed me deeply, which elicited a typi-cally male response. As if it was the answer she had been looking for, she pushed my door closed with one of her long, slender legs and then deftly rolled on top of me in the bed.

My left hand trailed from her neck down her back. In between passionate kisses, I came up for air and said, "I like the way you say thank you."

It turned out to be a spectacular Thursday night.

Chapter 13

My internal clock woke me a little late at 6:34 AM.

Amber was next to me, lightly snoring. I gently pulled myself away from her and slid out of bed. I grabbed my pants, shoes, and a shirt and snuck out of the room in search of civilization.

I nosed around the bay and found what looked like a community kitchen in between two other rooms. "Ah-ha, civilization. I found the coffee," I said to myself in an excited, quiet whisper. A few minutes later, I had a cup of hot coffee in each hand and headed back to my room. I pushed the door open, and Amber looked up at me.

"I hope one of those cups is coffee and that it's for me," she said with a sultry smile and her sexy hair strewn about her shoulders.

I smiled and stepped into the room as she sat up on the bed, taking the cup out of my left hand.

We sat together, drinking coffee and sharing perspectives about our past. Being with Amber was nice. It happened so fast I didn't even have time to get in my own way.

After our coffee was gone, Amber indicated it was time to get moving, so we got up, got dressed, and met in the lab with Orb-Quartz. After we'd discussed the plan's details, Orb-Quartz said, "Okay, it's time. Amber, make the call."

I watched Amber pace back and forth in the lab as she called her father and told him she was at the riverside off-site. She periodically glanced at me but stayed focused on her conversation. A few minutes later, she set her phone down and looked back toward Orb-Quartz and me.

"Okay, it's done. I let him know where I am," said Amber.

"Did he ask any questions?" asked Orb-Quartz

"Yes, he asked what I was doing. Specifically, whether I was alone and when I intended to depart. I'm sure you heard me give him the planned answers. He indicated that he may stop by shortly to understand what I was concerned about and complete his monthly facilities check."

"Hmmm, okay, that's not too unusual. Amber, please double-check the alarm. That's one thing I cannot do from here. We don't want to be surprised."

"Okay," she said as she looked at me with a closed-mouth smile on her face then turned to head out the lab's door.

"Quartz, are there others like you here?"

"Others like me? Not permanent residents, my brother and I are the only Peratholians in this region. Dr. Drake works for our government. He's a Peratholian scientist who visits periodically. He's leading the Project Renaissance effort for our government. We host a few other Peratholian visitors from time to time, but everyone else is human. My brother, Flint, Jessica, and Amber are the only ones who know about the Nexus Cores containing our minds and how the system works. Other employees understand they are important devices but don't know the details."

"Peratholian, is that what you are called?" I asked.

"Yes. Well, that's an English language version of it," Quartz replied.

"So Rockwell. Why did you hire him and expose your situation to a non-family member? That seems risky."

"It's complicated, Jack. The bottom line is that the stockpile of cloned Peratholian bodies my people created is gone, and we are having difficulty restarting the cloning process to create more. The process our ancestors used isn't working, so we brought in Rockwell to get an outside perspective. Rockwell has a superb genetics background and even possesses some neurobiology experience. He's under NDA not to disclose our cloning issue, and of course we are paying him well. I was keeping a close eye on him though. I wanted to be certain to keep the NeuraSync technology away from him."

Amber walked back into the lab, returning from her check on the alarm system.

"Jack, we need to be prepared for alternative courses of action. I recommend you hide your things and make it appear as if Amber is here alone in case others show up unexpectedly. Also, look in the brown metal security cabinet by the kitchen. There should be some restraints we can optionally use on Quartz and anyone else who shows up."

"Right, that makes sense," I said as I glanced at Amber, who now had an apprehensive look. "Everything will work out, Amber," I said as I turned and exited the lab and went into the main bay to hide my go bag and gather some needed items.

About forty minutes and two cups of coffee later, a black SUV rolled into the driveway and parked next to Amber's car.

"Jack!" Amber called out from the lab across the bay from the small kitchen.

"On my way," I replied as I dumped the coffee and hid the cup at the top of the cupboard.

I jogged to the lab, where Amber motioned me to look at the

remote camera screen, which depicted two people getting out of the SUV.

One was Quartz, and the other was a human named Don, who was huge.

"Okay, it looks like he brought Don from his security detail," said Orb-Quartz.

"I hope that's it. What are the odds he dropped others off up the driveway, out of view of the security camera?" I posited.

"Unknown, Jack. But there's only one way into this facility, so if we can control the door, the plan can still work. Don isn't a bad actor. If you can keep from shooting him, that would be ideal."

Shooting him? Shit. I'm a police officer. I'm not shooting anyone, I thought as I double-checked my pistol and the Taser. I was getting that feeling again of being used.

A loud pounding sound came from the locked bay door. Quartz or Don must have tried to open it and realized the deadbolt was set.

Amber's phone rang. She answered, "Hi, Dad. Yes, I'll come and open the door. Sorry, I forgot that I'd locked it."

She hung up the phone, and I followed her to the door and took up position, hiding in a utility closet around the corner from the door.

I could hear footsteps as one person entered the room and stopped to be greeted by Amber.

I heard Quartz's deep voice as he addressed her. "Amber, why are you here? This is very unusual."

I could faintly hear Amber's voice as she started to explain. Then I heard Quartz's voice once again, apparently talking to Don. "All secure inside. No issues. I'll be out in a few minutes."

Good. I thought, *hopefully, he's warned off Don.*

My heart pounded furiously as I took a step and started slinking around the corner of the closet.

As I pushed the door open, it freakin' creaked audibly. I could see Quartz standing with his back to me at least six meters away as he and Amber stood near the bay room door. Quartz must have heard the creak, as he suddenly jerked his head around and looked at me.

"Dammit!" he said as he reached out with his right arm and aggressively pushed Amber away from him with one swift motion.

"Stop, Quartz! I'm the police!" I yelled as he unholstered a pistol and fired it at me.

His bullet grazed my right bicep, causing me to drop the TASER X26P before I could pull the trigger.

Aiming the Taser was not easy at this range, as it wasn't really designed for shooting accurately at a distance. Aiming it with a wounded arm, when it was lying on the floor to boot, was going to be even more difficult.

Amber had gathered herself and leaped forward, grabbing Quartz's gun arm.

I sprinted forward, taking three steps, and lunged into Quartz as he'd pushed Amber away again. I took him down to the floor but suddenly realized how big and powerful the guy really was. He easily pushed me aside. We wrestled on the ground, and I whipped my left arm down across his body to break his grip on me. In a well-rehearsed move from my Army days, I used my left hand to grip his right arm and whipped my right arm across his face in a powerful elbow strike, targeting his chin. It struck home and slowed him, but he continued pushing me up and eventually threw me off. I rolled away and got to my feet as he reached for his pistol, which was on the ground, just out of his left hand's reach, so I stepped to the right and kicked his pistol along the bay floor.

The main bay door opened, and I turned to see Big Don walk into the bay.

Well hell, I thought.

"You shouldn't have involved yourself in this, Detective," said Quartz as he deftly swung a leg forward and kicked both of my legs out from under me, knocking me back to the ground, facing up in Don's direction as he walked toward me.

I pulled my Glock out of its holster and pointed it at Don as, from my peripheral vision, I saw Quartz, who had gotten to his feet, move in on me.

"Freeze, Don. I'm a police officer. Stop right there and raise your hands," I said before Quartz stepped over and kicked me in the ribs on my left side.

That kick hurt badly, and I rolled away, losing sight of Don.

I rolled to a kneeling position and pointed my pistol at Quartz and then at Don, saying, "Stop, both of you! I'm a police officer, and you are under arrest."

They seemed to consider my words as they both stopped moving forward for a moment.

Don pulled out a pistol, and I thought I'd have no choice but to shoot him.

Orb-Quartz's voice came over the bay's speaker system "Don, lower your weapon and stand fast. Do not involve yourself in this police action."

Don stopped, looking up toward the speakers, and lowered his weapon a few inches, so I turned back to face Quartz as he lunged forward, taking me painfully back to the floor. An incredibly powerful burst of pain erupted across my body as Quartz collapsed onto me. The physical pain was coming from everywhere at once. It was searing through my arms and chest. I was immobilized. What seemed like a minute elapsed as I tried to gather myself.

Dazed and confused, I thought I could see Amber's upside-down face hover over mine and faintly heard her say, "Jack, are you okay? Jack!"

She had dragged Quartz's body partially off of me, and as scrambled as my brain felt, I could distantly hear her explaining that she'd shot Quartz with the TASER on its highest setting, which affected me as well since we had been grappling with each other.

I started to recover.

"Don, stop," Orb-Quartz said over the speakers in the bay room's ceiling. I immediately looked in Don's direction and said, "Hold my gun on Don. If he moves, shoot him."

Amber picked up my Glock and pointed it in Don's direction, and then, surprising even me, she fired it in his direction, purposely missing but letting him know she would pull the trigger.

A perplexed Don froze and slowly raised his hands in a surrender motion while the pistol spun on his finger, which was protruding through the trigger guard, and pointed toward the ground.

I recovered enough to get out from under Quartz's body, then I stumbled over to Don and took his pistol, checking it to see how many rounds he had in the old six-shooter.

All six left, okay.

I put the pistol in my belt, handcuffed him with hands behind his back, and took him into one of the adjacent bedrooms.

Don asked me, "Why is Amber helping you detain Quartz?"

I locked his cuffs to the bed using a small chain and lock that

I'd found in the utility closet. "It's complicated, Don. Relax, it'll all make sense shortly." He peered up at me with uncertainty in his eyes. I wrapped a bandage around my bicep. *Luckily, Quartz just nicked me,* I thought.

"Jack!" Amber yelled. "We need to get him into the lab."

I jogged over to where she was standing.

"Right, let's do it," I said as I leaned over and picked Quartz up. I adjusted his body and put his left arm over my shoulder, basically dragging him into the lab room.

"Here, put him on this table."

Amber and I laid him on his back atop the thin table. She strapped on restraints so he couldn't move his arms or legs.

"I'm powering up the system," said Orb-Quartz.

The whole building seemed to rumble deeply as if a huge apparatus of some kind was slowly winding up. The thin table was connected to what looked like an old, densely wired MRI machine.

"Here, Jack. Turn this wheel. This will roll the table forward, positioning his head in the NeuraSync's induction chamber."

I nodded as Amber cleaned Quartz's arm and then stuck a needle into it. She completed the process by attaching the rest of the IV to Quartz's arm. That too was connected to the machine.

As she worked, the machine hummed to life with a number of lights and old-fashioned-looking meters fluctuating. Amber then attached a crown-looking device over Quartz's skull and connected it to even more wire junctions on the NeuraSync machine. "Okay, I think he's ready," said Amber. "I've given him the medicine."

Amber worked on the system, adjusting settings and talking with Orb-Quartz. "Amber, can you please double-check the inductive ground to ensure I do not receive his memories as input? I can't tell if it's properly in place."

Disappointing, I thought. I really wanted to know if Quartz's body had killed Jessica Frontage. I suppose he found something in the memory chip last night that gave him pause, at least enough to avoid receiving the inputs from Quartz's brain.

"Yes, let me double-check it. You should see a failsafe function return code of 8911. Is that what you see?"

"Yes. Well. It looks like we are ready. Jack, I know you wanted to know conclusively if Quartz killed Jessica, but I think there's another path to identifying Jessica's killer."

"Okay," I said glumly. "It would have been good to know, but I understand your concerns."

"Amber, best if you give Don an injection of midazolam to erase his memory. Jack, if you then could use your credentials to help Don understand what's going on in a positive way, it would be great. Don's a good man, and I need his loyalty moving forward despite this confusing situation."

Amber nodded at the wall camera connected to Orb-Quartz. "Okay, I'll take care of it."

"Yes," I replied. "I'll work with Don to ensure we don't create a mess."

"Thank you. I'll talk to you both in a few hours."

I looked at Amber and then up to Orb-Quartz's camera and nodded. "See you soon, Quartz."

"Jack, thank you for what you've done to save me. I'm very grateful, and I hope to make it up to you."

"No problem, Quartz. We'll keep our deal as is."

The neural induction machine started whining loudly, and Amber motioned for us to leave the lab.

"What if Quartz wakes up during the procedure?" I asked, following her back into the bay.

"He won't. Those chemicals keep him in a special state, so he cannot do anything to disrupt the NeuraSync's transfer process."

"It's amazing technology. How did you learn all this?" I asked.

"It's actually ancient technology, mostly analog in nature. My mother and father taught me all about the system. Now, my father and Flint trust me to take care of them with it. Besides them, I'm the only one who knows how to manage and operate the complete architecture."

I nodded and smiled, saying, "Well, it's certainly a lot of responsibility. You handle it well."

Amber smiled at me and said, "Why don't you get Don some water? I'll get a sedative to calm him down. Don is a good man, but I'm pretty sure he's very confused right now."

I smiled and said, "Well, you shooting at him isn't going to inspire future confidence."

Amber put her hands on her hips and gave me the side-eye as I raised my hands in a surrender motion. Then I nodded affirmatively, smiled, and started toward the small kitchen to get Don a bottle of water.

"It's going to be a while. Better break out the junk food we got last night. I'm starving," Amber said.

Chapter 14

Quartz sat up on the NeuraSync's narrow table a few hours later.

He looked around the room and then stood up as he rubbed his wrists.

Amber stood nearby and asked him a few questions, which he quietly answered.

"Hello, Jack," he said, looking in my direction.

I noticed his eyes were badly bloodshot, and he had a trickle of blood running from two spots on his head where Amber had removed the system's crown-like device.

I placed a hand on my pistol and replied, "Quartz, what was the frequency of the radio I used to hear you the very first time we met?"

Several seconds elapsed.

"700 Kilohertz, Jack. WLW, Cincinnati Reds baseball, that whole thing."

Amber was concerned as she turned to look at me. "He's okay, Jack. The correct neural network is in place in his brain."

Not satisfied, I asked a second question, "What was the name of the girl I had with me when we first met?"

Quartz replied immediately, "Ginger."

"Okay. Good. I haven't been certain about who's who recently," I said with obvious relief in my voice.

I walked over to Quartz and peered at him closely. "Your eyes look rough, and you're bleeding. You sure he's okay, Amber?"

Before Amber could reply, Quartz said, "It's fine, Jack. It's a common result during prolonged sync sessions. Burst vessels in the eyes are typical and will clear up in a day or two. Our eyeball tissue is especially resilient. This bleeding here on the head is superficial. It happens because of the amount of energy pushed through the NeuraSync's crown into the skull to transfer the neural network bits."

"Got it. Okay," I said as I nodded and looked over at Amber, who was beaming. Her eyes sparkled, as she was obviously happy to have her father back.

"It's good to have you back, Dad. It's been a long couple of days," she said with a smile.

"I completely understand. I'm glad to be back," he replied with an exhausted smile. "Now. It's time to get my headquarters back." Quartz powered his cell phone back on and noticed two messages. "Looks like I've been missed," he said as he dialed one of the missed call numbers. "Brother, what's going on?" A rapid-fire conversation between Quartz and his brother Flint ensued, and when Quartz ended the call, he looked like he was thinking hard about something. "We've got to go. The Carpathians are arriving soon to conduct our bi-annual planning meeting. I need to be there by 2 PM."

"Carpathians?" I queried.

"Yes. Think of them as other tribes. We are unified in our government, but the differing tribes live in various parts of our homeland and have differing cultures. The Carpathians also live in North America, so we meet periodically to work on common problems, such as the lack of cloned bodies." Quartz paced back in forth in the lab area as Amber stepped backwards, getting closer to me giving him room to maneuver.

He paused and turned to look at me. "Jack, can you please do me one more favor?"

I raised my eyebrows and gave him the side-eye. With a cautious tone, I said, "And what would that be?"

"If you could take my Nexus Core and hold it at the police station for a few days until I have a chance to sort this situation out, I'd be grateful. I need to be sure about its security in the near term."

I thought about what he'd asked, and after several long seconds of contemplation, I replied, "What's driving that request?" And then, without giving him a chance to answer, I continued, "Okay, I'll hold on to it for a couple of days. I'm headed that way now, so I'll take it."

He nodded and said, "Thank you, Jack. The information on that chip that you gave me last night showed how the NeuraSync could be used to overwrite another clone's matrix despite the preventative controls in place. I'm extremely grateful you shared it with me."

Quartz had convinced Big Don that all was well and that I was instrumental in helping him get the security situation back under control. Apparently, Don was good with the explanation. He gave me a hearty handshake prior to our departure, and a look of confidence had returned, indicating he was in good shape.

We all moved out.

Quartz and Don departed in their vehicle, heading back to Storm and Shield's headquarters.

I texted Chief Borland to let him know I'd be at the police station shortly as Amber was driving me back into town and dropping me at my truck, which was still parked at Green's Gym.

The chief seemed happy to hear I'd be there soon and said he'd track me down when I arrived. He said he'd bring good news and coffee.

Clem phoned as we drove into town. "Hi, Clem, good to hear from you. Everything okay?"

"Hi, Jack. Mostly okay. One odd thing I found with these murder victims. I wanted to double-check before I let you know. It's...very screwy."

"What is it, Clem? Lay it on me."

"Well, all the bodies we've found so far seem to be related."

"Related? What do you mean."

"Related, Jack. They have very similar DNA with specific differences in expression. All of them. The bodies found with Jessica Frontage and the two at the golf course."

"Hmmm, okay, are they related to Jessica Frontage?"

"Nope, she's the outlier. It's weird, especially given their distributed age range. It's like someone murdered an entire family and ditched them separately. I sure hope this isn't a Wellspoint family, Jack."

"Let's hope that theory is incorrect, Clem. I'll add it to the report. Can you send me some of the technical details?"

"Will do, Jack. Man, I hope you guys can figure out who's killing all these people."

"Me too, Clem, me too. Thanks. I will stop by on Monday to discuss."

"Okay, have a good weekend."

"You too."

When we arrived at my truck, Amber turned to me and gave me a smolderingly sexy smile.

Her smile transitioned into a pensive, solemn stare, and she said, "You are very special, Jack. I've not been able to have a relationship with anyone who could know who my father really is. I've never seen him trust a human like he trusts you."

With that, she leaned forward, placing a hand on each side of my face, and kissed me. It was the most passionate, deep kiss I've ever experienced! I was mesmerized. She pulled away from me and smiled with that gleam in her eye, indicating she was considering something wickedly fun. Finally, I managed to snap out of it. "I'll give you a call, Amber. Maybe we can catch a baseball game sometime."

She tilted her head a degree and smiled broadly, saying, "Anytime, Jack Stewart, anytime."

* * *

I attracted some strange looks as I walked into the police station on that fateful Friday afternoon. When I stopped in the restroom, I noticed why. I was sporting a slightly bruised right eye and a cut on my chin. That, coupled with a two-day beard, unkempt hair, and a very wrinkled shirt, resulted in a shabby-looking detective. I looked like shit. And that was unusual. So people noticed. I washed my face, ran some water through my hair, and then used about a hundred paper towels to dry myself off.

Schultzy came into the bathroom and stood at one of the urinals. "Rough night, sir? You look like hell," he said with a smile. Then he turned to face me and said, "Chief's been waiting for you. You know, we have showers down in the gym," Schultzy said with his typical humorous and sarcastic tone.

"Hi, Schultzy," I said. "Yes, but then I'd have to work out, right? Isn't that the rule?"

"I think so, Detective. Yes, that's the rule."

I checked in the mirror again. *Well, I don't look much better, but I do feel refreshed,* I thought. "Have a good rest of your Friday,

Schutlzy."

"Thanks, you too, Detective."

I found my way to my office, pulled Orb-Quartz out of my coat pocket, and placed him into my go-bag. I stepped up onto my chair and then onto my desk. "Quartz," I said, "I need to hide you in the ceiling for a while. I will collect you shortly. I'll turn my radio on and keep it at a low volume, so give me a shout if you need to chat."

Orb-Quartz acknowledged and again offered his gratitude for keeping the electronic version of himself safely out of reach for a while.

I pushed a specific ceiling tile aside, revealing my hiding place for small things. I hid the go-bag in a small space in the ceiling, replaced the ceiling tile, and jumped down from the desk. *I doubt Orb-Quartz can get into too much trouble from up here*, I thought. I sat down and logged into my computer to start writing this report. It was going to take a while.

Fifteen minutes into my report, the chief, holding a cup of coffee that looked to be very cold, came into my office.

"Welcome back, Jack. Schultzy mentioned that you'd returned," he said with a grin. "Come on, I need to meet with you in the vault."

The vault was a secure room where we handled sensitive investigation activities, particularly those involving undercover officers. There were few computers, and the files couldn't be removed from the room.

"Hi, Chief, good to see you. Okay, that sounds good. I've got a lot of updates for you on the Jessica Frontage murder case," I said as I stood and walked toward the door. "Can we stop for coffee along the way?"

We small-talked our way to the operations center's coffee

pot. I grabbed a cup of coffee as the chief freshened his cup. I noticed that the W-shaped birthmark on his right hand was, again, missing. My mind immediately started wheeling through dark scenarios where a clone had replaced the chief. I tried to remain calm as I reeled through the list of people I thought I could genuinely trust. Unfortunately, it was a short list.

As we entered the vault room, the chief said, "Jack, this is Amanda Seward. She's the chief of the bureau's Special Action Group."

I took a look at the other occupant of the vault. Amanda had an average build and stood about 5' 10". She had dark hair and brown eyes.

"Hi, Jack, it's great to meet you," she said as she stood, stepping toward me and smiling as she offered her hand to shake.

I leaned forward and took her outstretched hand. "It's good to meet you as well. Chief tells me great things about you and your team."

Chief started, "Mandy's got some info that I think will help us with the Jessica Frontage case. I think it will also help us in dealing with the folks over at Storm and Shield."

I smiled uncomfortably as we all took seats at the small table. I was troubled by the eerie possibility that Chief Borland wasn't the Chief Borland I knew and he somehow didn't know it. Or, worse yet, that he was involved in Jessica Frontage's murder. *Lots of things to work through*, I thought, trying to look relaxed.

"First things first," Mandy started, "all of this is classified. It cannot leave this room. Jack, I need you to sign a non-disclosure agreement."

She passed me the form, and I read through it briefly. Apparently, this project was called "Copper Jackal" by the folks in the bureau, as that title was stamped at the top and bottom of the NDA.

After signing the document, I slid it back over to her and said, "Okay, here you go."

She looked at the chief, and he gave her a single nod of approval.

"Jack, about twelve weeks ago, a bureau informant within the Storm and Shield headquarters staff was murdered," Mandy started.

"Jessica Frontage," I replied with a deadpan voice.

"Yes, Jack, that's right. She initially came to us about eight months ago. She was working with scientists at Storm and Shield, who were deep into experimenting with cloning. They worked on cloning several species of animals and even an extinct species of early humans. However, that cloning effort suddenly shifted to a focus on cloning humans. Jessica didn't like it and thought it was the start of a path that could be bad for Storm and Shield and perhaps humanity itself. Somewhere along the path, we think she discovered something significant. It was significant enough to get her killed. I have a few more bits to share, but do you have any questions or comments before we continue?"

I contemplated this new information, and it did prompt a question. "Okay. Did we do an autopsy on Jessica?" I asked.

"Yes. Not much there," Mandy said as she shuffled through some more papers, finding the one she was looking for. "Okay, here we go. There was no blunt force trauma or life-threatening wounds found on her body. The only remarkable issue was severely bloodshot eyes. It says numerous vessels burst in her eyes, but there was no skin tissue bruising around the eyes. Very odd."

I considered her thoughts as the chief jumped in. "Jack, apparently they are not aliens, as I originally suspected. They are, however, a different species of humans."

"They call themselves Peratholians," Mandy said, "They were apparently here before us modern humans. The continent of Antarctica is their original homeland. And they have spread out and sparsely populated three or four countries in the past nine hundred years."

"How many live in the United States?" I asked.

"We are not certain, but according to the classified reports, there are less than fifty living among humans globally."

"Okay. Well, it's good to know the bureau is tracking these people, as I had no idea they existed before this case."

"It's a closely held government secret, Jack. There's some sort of high-level agreement that exchanges tech with their species for some kind of cohabitation rights," Mandy said as she smiled tightly. "The 'cloning humans' part is a big deal because, apparently, the Peratholians have run out of their stockpile of cloned bodies. As you and Chief Borland are aware, they've lived for centuries by transferring knowledge from their electronic brains, called Nexuses, into the cloned bodies. Then, after a few weeks of activity, they transfer the new experiences from the body back into the Nexus device. Their clone bodies are quite resilient. They can last for hundreds of years."

"Yes," I replied, "I'm tracking that part. They apparently need to sync their body with their Nexus Core device using the NeuraSync thing every few weeks, or the clone body's cognitive function is degraded."

Mandy nodded affirmatively, saying, "Jack, it would be devastating if another species started cloning humans to use as hosts or, worse, taking over non-cloned human brains. Who knows what they could be capable of?"

"Yes, agreed, this human cloning has to be stopped. Who knows how far they are in this process? We need more answers."

Mandy nodded in agreement as Chief Borland took over the conversation.

"Jack, I originally asserted that Quartz had killed Jessica Frontage. However, Mandy here was just informing me that Quartz is Jessica's stepfather. I guess he had a relationship with this woman..." The chief fumbled through several documents and finally found the one he was looking for and slid it my way on the table. "Isabella Garcia. Her maiden name was Frontage. She's a modern human, obviously."

I looked at the picture of Isabella. There was definitely a resemblance between this woman and both Jessica and Amber. *Well, this at least confirms part of what Quartz told me about his past,* I thought.

Mandy continued, "Jessica came to work with Quartz after her mother, Isabella, died about nine years ago. She didn't want anyone to know that she was Quartz's stepdaughter. Apparently, Jessica had some bad relationship experiences and a run-in with substance abuse. She was looking for a fresh start. Quartz helped by giving her that start."

Mandy's eyes widened with a look of earnestness as she peered at the chief and then back to me, saying, "I'd met with Jessica personally several times. She always commented on how kind and generous Quartz was to her. Apparently, he helped her through a very difficult part of her life. So when Chief Borland told me this morning that he made Quartz for the murderer, I had to come over and provide some background. Not saying it's impossible, but it seems unlikely based on her statements."

"Yes," I said, "it's good to have your information as we try and judge the situation." I looked to the chief. "I'm certain no one wants to get it wrong when it comes to finding her killer." We sat quietly for a few seconds.

When the chief didn't respond, I decided to change the subject.

I looked at Mandy and asked, "Did Jessica ever say anything about old friends, new relationships? Love interests?"

"In our second-to-last session, she mentioned that she'd started a relationship with a coworker at Storm and Shield. She was definitely smitten. I have his picture here somewhere." She shuffled through the file and found the item she wanted. "Here he is. Dr. Alexander Rockwell. Smart guy. And capable, according to Jessica. Apparently, he's a geneticist and has a background in neurobiology. When we checked him out though, we found he'd left his previous gig under a cloud of suspicion. Something regarding unethical experimentation. We tried but were not able to find more details there. Maybe he's helping the Peratholians with the cloning of humans. We are not sure."

I took the picture from her and looked at it. I recognized this guy right away. "Chief, this is the guy who came out of Storm and Shield on Tuesday. He exited about thirty minutes before you blasted through the main Storm and Shield doors. They got into a car and took off. He didn't seem to be in a hurry either."

Chief Borland looked from me to Mandy and, with a sheepish expression, replied, "That morning is still hazy for me, Jack."

"This picture of Rockwell," I said, pointing at the photo, "this person with him looks like Jessica Frontage."

"Yes. One of my agents took surveillance photos of the two having dinner at a restaurant downtown."

Boom. Everything suddenly clicked together in my mind. "This is the guy. I think we need to arrest him for the murder of Jessica Frontage."

"What?" Mandy asked.

"Jack, can you run through your theory with us?" said Chief Borland with a lilt of respectful disbelief in his voice.

Mandy and the chief looked at me with puzzled concern as I continued. "Quartz told me that severely bloodshot eyes or burst vessels were common with long sync sessions in their NeuraSync system."

"So you think Rockwell drugged her and used the NeuraSync on her? Why would he do that? It doesn't work on regular humans, right?"

We sat in silence for nearly a minute before I continued, "Something's new there, especially if they are cloning humans to put their neural networks into. Besides, if he found out she was talking to the police, he would be incentivized to cut that off to stop us from finding out about their human cloning activities. Cloning humans is illegal. I think he forced her to do a session in the NeuraSync, or maybe voluntarily. He could have tricked her into it and used it to kill her. To shut her up. Somehow, he applied the neural network modifications to her brain in a way that killed her. Maybe over-juiced it."

"Murder by neural network?" asked Chief Borland.

"I think so. Quartz told me that without consistent use by the NeuraSync, degenerative diseases could rapidly set in. The brain evolves to depend on that NeuraSync thing. One of the worst types is a disease similar to accelerated ALS that impacts breathing, heart, and other key organ functions. Maybe they figured out how to make it generate those effects in humans. There are also intravenous drugs used during the procedure. Perhaps something there contributed."

"Toxicology report came up empty for drugs, Jack," replied Chief Borland.

I nodded knowingly. "Okay, that's good." I considered all the events and all the evidence. "Shit," I said, "Quartz is probably walking into a trap. Doctor Rockwell or the Carpathians must be the ones manipulating Quartz and Flint. Quartz indicated that he was aware of new technology that could overwrite the neural network in the Nexus thing."

"Who are the Carpathians? And why would they want to manipulate Quartz and Flint? To control what they think about something?" asked the chief.

Mandy broke in, "The Carpathians are a different family of Peratholians from Quartz and Flint. They are all the same species but originate from differing regions of the Antarctic. They hold government meetings together at specified intervals."

I nodded affirmatively. "And as to why they would want to manipulate Quartz and Flint, well, it probably has something to do with this new activity—cloning of humans. My guess is Quartz wouldn't support it. He seems very principled. And he never mentioned knowing about human cloning activities. So maybe the Carpathians are trying to coerce Quartz and Flint into agreeing with human cloning and generating new bodies for themselves."

A short period of quiet thinking overtook the three of us.

Chief Borland reached into his pocket and showed me a folded piece of paper.

"Two hours ago, I received the search warrant approval from the judge for Storm and Shield's headquarters building."

I stood and said, "Excellent. Well, there are two things we need to do. Let's go arrest this Rockwell guy for murdering Jessica Frontage and put a stop to whoever is cloning humans."

"Let's do it," the chief replied.

Chief Borland and I stood and stepped toward the door, and then I stopped and looked back at Mandy. "Are you coming?"

She shook her head and said she didn't want to show her face at that location, as it might compromise other ongoing activities.

I didn't know what that was about, but I thanked her earnestly for sharing her information. I felt better about the chief, but I still didn't think it was a good time to inform him about the Chief Borland clone I had seen in the basement of Storm and Shield. I can't get the birthmark issue out of my head.

On our way out, the chief stopped and gave some instructions to the operations sergeant and two additional police officers. We made a simple plan and then bolted for my car.

Chapter 15

The chief and I took off in my car, hoping we would be in time for, well, we weren't sure what we would find waiting for us at the offices of Storm and Shield.

But, across town, almost as if they knew we were coming, a meeting was taking place.

***

Quartz and Big Don walked into the rear entryway of Storm and Shield's headquarters building after parking in their private lot. This access had less security because of the parking lot's security controls.

Flint greeted Quartz and Don as they walked into the main hallway. "Good to see you, brother. I was worried when I couldn't reach you this morning."

Quartz forced a calm smile and replied, "Sorry, I was busy with a friend. Can you please go over the situation with me?"

"Yes, the Carpathians want to discuss the latest cloning results with you. They...have some ethical concerns and—"

"And what?"

"Well, Victor Drake's presence has them rattled."

"Drake is here for the meeting?"

"Yes."

"Interesting. Okay, well, he is in charge of Project Renaissance."

Quartz contemplated his next move. He needed information about Jessica but had to be careful about how he asked for it. "Brother, there's a lot of scrutiny over Jessica Frontage's death. I'd like to know your thoughts on it again."

"Quartz, I swear, my team had nothing to do with it. I'm very sorry she passed but don't have any details on how or why it occurred. Did the police tell you anything about her condition?"

Quartz was pensive, staring off into the distance as he thought. "The only information I have is that she didn't have any major wounds and did not seem to be poisoned. I just don't know, but I do intend to find out. Her death is on me. Her mother would have been so disappointed."

Flint put his right hand on Quartz's shoulder. "Try not to be so hard on yourself, Quartz. She had a troubled past. It's possible something there crept back in." Quartz nodded, but Flint could see the emotion this scenario had churned up in his brother. "Brother, we have some time before the meeting starts. Come on, let me get you a coffee and something to eat. We've got some fresh blueberry and carrot cake muffins. You look like you could use a snack."

Quartz was clearly still wheeling through several thoughts but finally looked at his brother and then nodded affirmatively and said, "Yes, that does sound good. I am a bit hungry. But first I need to look at the computer logs from a few weeks back. I also need to tell you about my Nexus. Come on, let's go."

Twenty minutes later, Quartz and Flint entered the conference room.

Quartz instructed Big Don to wait outside the conference room doors as he didn't want Don to participate in the discussion.

Two Carpathians walked into the room a few minutes later

and stopped to greet Quartz and Flint. They were a couple, Cloee and Adam Tholl. She was a scientist and was working closely with their limited government in the Antarctic to revitalize their cloning program.

Quartz and Flint both recognized them and politely welcomed them to the facility.

"I must say, Quartz, the progress Drake has made in working with your Dr. Rockwell is amazing, if not frightening. I was surprised to hear that you allowed, even promoted, the experiments."

Quartz looked at Cloee with a forced smile and said, "That's what I want to talk about. Apparently, Drake has a breakthrough that he wishes to discuss with us during the session. I, on the other hand, am catching up a bit." Quartz looked over at Flint.

"My brother was just telling me that he'd finally recovered his Nexus after it was stolen months ago during an incident. He re-synced this morning but is still working to restore some of his memories."

Cloee and Adam looked at one another and then at Quartz.

"Why didn't you inform us of this? There are only three families of Peratholians in North America. All are protected by covenant with the American government."

"Because," Flint replied, "there is also an investigation. One of our employees died unexpectedly. The police suspected murder and brought Quartz in for questioning a few times. We were hoping to get everything resolved before this session."

Three humans entered the room and started setting up computers and a projector. One of them was Dr. Alexander Rockwell. "If everyone could please take their seats," said the dark-haired human who Quartz didn't recognize.

Flint, Quartz, and the Carpathians sat at the table.

"It's good to see you, Quartz," said the dark-haired human.

Quartz glanced at Flint with a look of curiosity.

Flint looked from Quartz to the Carpathians and finally back to the human.

"Drake, I should have mentioned this before now. Quartz's Nexus Core was stolen several months ago and was just recovered this week. Quartz re-synced this morning and is having trouble reconciling some of his memories."

The man, apparently named Drake, looked at Quartz with concern as the blond-haired man seated next to him suddenly stood up.

"Drake? Is that you? In a human body?" Quartz said flatly as he realized Drake was in the dark-haired man's body.

"Quartz, we've been through this. You agreed to support our experimentation. You agreed that—"

"I would never have agreed to this," Quartz's deep voice boomed as he interrupted Drake.

"Drake, we agreed to test," said Cloee, "testing our accelerated cloning algorithms to start creating new Peratholian clones from new genetic resourcing. Quartz and I never agreed to clone, especially NeuraSync transitions into modern human bodies. It's against the covenant."

Drake turned red with anger. "Oh, come on, Cloee, Quartz. What did you think we were going to do? Both of you. We are facing the end of our species, the end of our people. Our ancestors would have done this. Need I remind you we are out of clone bodies! Out. Every single attempt to restart the ancient cloning process has failed. Our nuclear genetic transfer no longer works. In every case, our new Peratholian clones grew into adults but did not function properly. We simply lack the genetic diversity needed to continue the process our ancestors used. Meanwhile, our society slips further into the shadows of existence."

The blond-haired man drew a pistol and aimed it at Quartz.

Quartz stood up quickly.

"Easy, Javin," said Drake.

"Javin Paulus," Quartz said.

"Yes," replied Javin.

"Take care pointing your pistol in my direction," said Quartz in a deeply threatening tone as he pulled back his jacket to reveal his own pistol.

"You don't frighten me, Quartz. This human body is less capable physically, but I'm still inside. I'll take you out in a blink of your aged Peratholian eyes."

"Gentlemen, please compose yourselves, Javin, Quartz. Please, everyone, sit down," said Dr. Alexander Rockwell.

"Dr. Rockwell's efforts were key to helping us overcome numerous challenges in using the NeuraSync with the human brain," said Drake with a proud yet irritated tone.

"The NeuraSync works on humans now? How have you done this? Human brains do not have the equivalent of the regaltus and pealtus components in our Peratholian brains," said Cloee.

"Alexander showed us how to inductively sum the network correlations from those two organs and implement a sort of mixer in the NeuraSync that can be used to overlay the right intermediate neural network layers within a specific part of the human brain's cerebellum. It compensates quite efficiently over time. The human brain requires more frequent NeuraSync sessions initially, but it seems to retain integrity far longer than our Peratholian brains."

A stunned hush fell over Quartz, Flint, and the Carpathians as they contemplated the sheer gravity of the moment. The end of their species was in sight, while the raw exploitation of another loomed in Quartz and Cloee's minds.

Finally, Quartz responded, "I don't like this. Where did you acquire those bodies? It's wrong."

Drake pointed to Javin and then back to himself. He replied, "The bodies belonged to nameless vagrants. They were willing participants and will not be missed."

"You took over their brains, destroying their existing minds? Is it reversible?"

"No, it's not *reversible*," declared Rockwell indignantly, "but it is a miracle for your people. Please, everyone, sit down. Javin, please put the pistol down."

Drake quickly took over. "Quartz, this is the way. Our Peratholian accelerated-cloning algorithm requires thousands of modifications to work on humans. The data shows that we are very close to finding one that works. It is much closer than cloning ourselves. But we needed to make the NeuraSync work on the human brain, and we've done that. From there, we'll focus on taking over cloned bodies. Our tests show that we'll be able to grow a human clone to maturity in five months with the right genetic material. This is the only way to save our species and puts us in a better position globally."

Chapter 16

Jack and Chief Borland entered the Storm and Shield headquarters building through the now-familiar front door.

They walked down the steps and were greeted by a security guard who stood from his desk.

"I'm Troy Borland, chief of Wellspoint Police. I have a warrant to search this facility in support of a murder investigation." We showed the guard our badges and the warrant.

The guard gestured for us to enter, and I could see Big Don in the distance, so I headed in his direction.

I walked up to Don and shook his hand. He asked me what was going on, and I replied that we'd gotten a warrant to search the premises for artifacts related to the Jessica Frontage murder.

Don got a worried look on his face, and I told him that everything would be okay and not to get jumpy. I told him that we were not after him or Quartz; we were looking for Alexander Rockwell.

Don indicated that Rockwell and everyone else who mattered was in the main conference room.

"Chief, our suspect is in the conference room," I said as the chief approached with the security guard in tow.

"Thanks, Jack. I gave Schultzy and Baker guidance to start looking through files in the administrative office. Let's go get

Rockwell."

I pulled the conference room doors open, and Chief Borland and I walked through them, drawing the attention of everyone in the room.

They were all seated around a large square table.

"Everyone, keep your seats and keep your hands where we can see them," said Chief Borland as we split up and walked toward opposite sides of the table.

We held our police badges high in our left hands, side arms down at our sides in our other hands.

"Jack, what is going on? I told you I would sort this out. Please leave," said Quartz, who was visibly irritated.

Before I could respond, Chief Borland said, "Everyone, stay calm. We are executing a search warrant as part of an ongoing murder investigation."

"You, Rockwell," I said and gestured at him, "are under arrest for the murder of Jessica Frontage. Stand up, place your hands on your head, and step toward me."

The words appeared to hit Rockwell like a hammer. "I didn't kill Jessica. I loved her!"

"You loved her enough to use the NeuraSync to kill her. Stand up, you son of a bitch!" I yelled at Rockwell.

He stood up and started lamenting. "I didn't kill her," he said to Drake. "Please tell them."

"Shut up," said Javin.

In the corner of my eyes, I saw Quartz's large frame stand up.

I turned in time to see Quartz draw his pistol and aim it in the direction of Rockwell. "Quartz!" I yelled, "Stand down. This is my show. Do not shoot Rockwell!"

Quartz replied, "Why did you kill that girl?"

"I swear, I didn't kill her," fretted Rockwell.

"Shut up!" Quartz yelled at him.

Slowly, Javin Paulus stood so that his hand could reach his pistol.

"Quartz," started Drake, "it was an unfortunate accident. Dr. Rockwell made a terrible mistake."

"No, it wasn't Rockwell. She found out about your human cloning efforts and decided to stop you. And when you found out about it, you had Javin use the NeuraSync to murder her so you could pin it on Rockwell and cover your tracks."

Rockwell looked from Quartz to Drake and finally to Javin.

"You assholes!" said Rockwell in the direction of both Javin and Drake.

"Quartz," pleaded Drake, "we are at a precipice. This is the turning point for our people. Would you have us die out?"

"Quartz, lower your pistol," I said in a low tone.

"Drake, Jessica was my stepdaughter, my wife's daughter before she met me. Her dying wish was for me to take care of her. So I brought her here to work for me and live a decent life. And you decided to murder her."

"Quartz, you can't prove any of this," Javin said. "Let it go. We don't have time for this."

"I checked the data from the lab closely. The NeruaSyncs consume predictably enormous amounts of energy during sync sessions. I saw numerous logs where Dr. Rockwell and Jessica went into the lab and executed limited NeuraSync sessions. The consumption of electricity aligns perfectly with those small uses. Somehow, the good doctor here convinced Jessica to use the system willingly."

"She wanted to participate in the research, but I never let her receive any network modulation data. Only read her brain's neural network. I never put the crown on her," said Rockwell with a strained and trembling voice.

"That makes sense, small, short bursts of electricity on the date and times you both were in the lab. But on the day of Jessica's murder, she came to work and never went home. Neither Flint nor I came to the headquarters building that day. You were here, Javin, and so were you, Drake. You convinced her to do a session. That session used a lot more electricity than before, consuming hundreds of kilowatts. You used the NeuraSync to insert nulled network connections into her brain. Her body simply stopped functioning, no heartbeat, no breathing. No evidence, nothing to connect to you."

In the blink of an eye, Javin Paulus retrieved his pistol and fired at Quartz.

His shot missed. His bullet struck the table in front of Quartz.

And that was because Quartz had shot him in the face with his Colt 1911 Pistol.

Javin slumped onto the table, blood spreading out from under his body and across the surface.

"You have your murderer, Jack," said Quartz without turning his head. He aimed his pistol at Drake. "Just as I promised."

"Quartz, lower the weapon," said Chief Borland calmly.

"Chief," Quartz said, " did you know that they intended to replace you with a clone? That's what happened to you on Tuesday morning."

Chief Borland turned briefly and looked in my direction.

"I think he's right. I saw what looked like a well-developed Chief Borland clone downstairs when I came in to reset Quartz's self-destruct mechanism. Tuesday morning, they must have drugged you and tried to use the NeuraSync on you, but those two metal plates in your head probably screwed up the NeuraSync. The machine did manage to screw you up though.

Bloodshot eyes, dizziness, memory issues, erratic behavior. You had it all."

"And when were you going to let me know about this?" asked the chief, looking at me with a perplexed, irritated expression.

"Right around the time I thought it could be helpful. Like now. And after I could confirm you were not involved," I replied.

Chief Borland looked back toward Drake and raised his pistol, pointing it in Drake's direction. "Hands on your head, you son of a bitch!"

"We are gods in these brains!" Drake screamed at Quartz as he reached for something from his bag on the table's surface. "This is our right, our destiny!"

Quartz ended Drake's tirade with a single bullet. Drake's body slumped onto the table and then fell to the floor.

Everyone lowered their weapons.

I slowly approached Quartz, who looked like a man who'd released all his anger into a punching bag. He looked exhausted. "It's over," said Quartz as he looked toward Flint, Cloee, and Adam.

They all nodded in agreement.

"This path is very dangerous. We must put controls in place to stop the overzealous from taking matters into their own hands," replied Cloee.

"You should have let me take him in, Quartz," I said. "Now I have another dead body to deal with."

"Forget it, Jack," Chief Borland said as he walked up to me. "Quartz has a right to self-defense. Besides, they'd already destroyed the minds of those bodies. And, these two are both probably backed up to a Nexus Core somewhere, so they aren't really dead."

I contemplated Chief Borland's words as he continued, "But

what about the other three bodies that were found with Jessica and the two bodies that were discovered at the golf course?" Chief Borland asked.

"Data from the computer downstairs indicates they were human clones. The NeuraSync didn't work properly on them," Quartz said. " Apparently, Drake's team has been busy. They've cloned dozens of humans, and some ended up having defects in their vital organs. It's a common challenge in cloning complex beings. Many of them were cloned elsewhere and brought here for NeuraSync testing."

"Yes, that tracks with what Clem found. He said all the dead bodies, except Jessica's, were closely related genetically, according to his DNA tests."

Chief Borland contemplated this and finally looked up at Quartz and said, "Quartz, this human cloning shit stops right here, right now. Your people can figure out another way. Our government can help with that—no more clandestine biological bullshit. Jack and I have been briefed on the program. We understand there's an agreement. I'm sure our people can work together to figure something out."

A weary, towering Quartz nodded thoughtfully in agreement. "Yes, Chief. Our people will find another way. Perhaps with the help of modern humans."

I jumped in, "Besides, if you can successfully procreate with modern humans like Isabella, then it's probably possible to leverage a hybrid solution for generating genetic materials and a more effective cloning process."

Quartz nodded with a smile and said, "Amber."

I nodded affirmatively at Quartz and then looked over to the chief.

"Amber, is your offspring, Quartz? That's amazing. That

must be a first for our people. Why did you keep it hidden from us?" asked Cloee.

"I wanted her to have a chance to grow up and live a normal life. She was Jessica's stepsister. We kept their relationship hidden from Amber, per Jessica's wishes, but I will tell her about it as soon as we get all this settled. They were close friends, and she has a right to know."

Chief Borland called in for the medical examiner and a few more policemen to get the situation under control.

When things slowed down and we'd collected all the data we needed, Quartz took Flint, Chief Borland, and me down into the project renaissance lab in the corner of the main lab facility. Flint was upset that he wasn't aware of all the activity occurring in the lab where Drake and Javin were conducting their research. Looking back, he blindly trusted them too much, and he was pretty sure it was Javin who tried to sabotage Quartz's Nexus Core.

"Don't be too hard on yourself, brother. You are the businessman in the family. Leaving the science and security to me is best for everyone," replied Quartz as he patted his brother on the back.

Standing in front of the massive tank, we all looked at Chief Borland's clone in silence as it floated there peacefully.

"So if we get rid of it, is that murder?" asked the chief.

"Despite its nearly adult size, it hasn't experienced anything and is really not alive in any truly human way. I think we should destroy it," said Quartz.

We all nodded in agreement as we stood around the tank, each musing about the disaster our efforts had averted.

I glanced over and finally got a close-up of the chief's right hand as he placed it on the tank next to me, watching the clone float about. It had the faintest outline of the W-shaped birthmark. *He must have gotten it treated*, I thought. It made me think about other loose ends.

"Chief, what are we going to do with Rockwell?" I asked. "He knows a great deal about what's going on and doesn't seem particularly trustworthy."

Quartz jumped in, "Jack, he's a Storm and Shield employee. I'll talk with him. I'll get him to agree to work from one of our sites in the Antarctic for a while. Pay him well. We'll see if we can make some use of his expertise. That and he'll be far away from home for a long time."

"Sounds like a good solution," replied the chief. "Hopefully that ties up all the loose ends."

"Speaking of loose ends," I asked the chief curiously, "I still can't figure out how you found Quartz's Nexus Core. You said it was with the bodies?"

"The forensics team found it wedged in the trunk of Jessica's car, down where the spare tire was located. Her trunk was loaded with odds and ends. Most likely, she'd hid it there long before she was murdered."

Quartz shook his head with amazement. "Jessica was such a sweetheart, protected me to the end. She's the hero in this story."

I considered all the events from a hectic four days' worth of activity and pondered my opportunities for relaxation with Amber. *I could use a long weekend,* I thought.

I considered my past and how events had shaped who I am. A regular guy. A detective working toward the greater good of society. All my frailties. All my strengths.

Our minds are so vulnerable to the wrong inputs. Have to keep that in mind from now on, I thought.

My mind drifted toward baseball. In all its purity, baseball made sense. At least to me.

With the murder of Jessica Frontage solved, things in lovely Wellspoint, Ohio, would hopefully start to get back to normal.

About the Author

M.A. Mollenkopf is a cyberspace security specialist who enjoys writing software and books.

As a boy, he was inspired by Robert Heinlein's Space Cadet novel and became an instant, lifelong fan of science fiction.

He is married and lives in Georgia with his wife.

You can reach out to him at **mamollenkopf@graviscape.net**

You can connect with me on:
https://twitter.com/almollenkopf

Also by M.A. Mollenkopf

The Graviscape: Unexpected Expedition
Captain Dave Murray and the crew of the Algonquin disappear from Earth's solar system during a vital Space Colonization Agency mission and find themselves reemerging light years away in a crowded planetary system with no weapons, no supplies and no way to return home.

Through first contact scenarios, the captain and crew discover the Graviscape, the only energy field that traverses all space-time dimensions. When properly modulated, data and even matter can be transported at faster-than-light speeds giving them a potential option to get home.

The civilian captain and crew must leverage their new partnerships to try and defeat the enemy's experienced military combat space fleet to save Earth from a devastating attack.

Partnerships are weaponized driving an unusual alignment of allies and enemies where loyalty and love are pitted against hate and uncertainty.

Science fiction fans that like adventure, first contact, battling one's inner monologue and emotional drama will love this epic journey, book #1 in the Graviscape storyline.

www.ingramcontent.com/pod-product-compliance
Lightning Source LLC
Chambersburg PA
CBHW071154300726
48975CB00004B/1145